I0607614

Beautiful in the Lord's Eyes

SOMETIMES, REAL BEAUTY SHINES
AFTER A TRAGEDY

Susan Kohler

CCB Publishing
British Columbia, Canada

Beautiful in the Lord's Eyes:
Sometimes, Real Beauty Shines After A Tragedy

Copyright ©2015 by Susan Kohler
ISBN-13   978-1-77143-230-6
First Edition

Library and Archives Canada Cataloguing in Publication
Kohler, Susan, 1950-, author
Beautiful in the lord's eyes : sometimes, real beauty shines after a tragedy
/ by Susan Kohler. -- First edition.
Issues in print and electronic formats.
ISBN 978-1-77143-230-6 (pbk.).--ISBN 978-1-77143-231-3 (pdf)
Additional cataloguing data available from Library and Archives Canada

Original cover art design by Ginny Glass: www.wordsugardesigns.com

The characters and events in this book are fictitious. Any similarity to real persons, living or dead, is coincidental and not intended by the author.

Extreme care has been taken by the author to ensure that all information presented in this book is accurate and up to date at the time of publishing. Neither the author nor the publisher can be held responsible for any errors or omissions. Additionally, neither is any liability assumed for damages resulting from the use of the information contained herein.

All rights reserved. No part of this publication may be reproduced, stored in a retrieval system or transmitted in any form or by any means, electronic, mechanical, photocopying, recording or otherwise without the express written permission of the publisher.

Publisher: CCB Publishing
             British Columbia, Canada
             www.ccbpublishing.com

Dedication

To the Lord God who saved and inspired me.

To my friends from Connection Pointe Church
who accepted me as one of them.

To Mike, Sable and Oreo who put up with me.

And to Paul and Jack for their help and advice.

Introduction

I want to put in a word about some of the characters in this book. They come from books I have published as Contemporary Romances. Although one of the books, *Dreaming of Tomorrow*, is based on my faith, it was not written as a Christian book but as a romance novel. Since Nicole was a secondary character in one of these books, I've used some of the characters from these books in this work.

All Bible verses are taken from the King James Version, Copyright 1987, which is in the Public Domain.

Chapter One

"We always thank God, the Father of our Lord Jesus Christ, praying always for you, since we have heard of your faith in Christ Jesus and of the love which ye have to all the saints."
(Colossians 1:3-4)

Nicole swirled around in the designer dress she was wearing, her long, blonde hair flowing with the rest of her body as she turned. The silky dress was floor length and flowing in bright yellows and pale greens. It had a dangerously low neckline, and a slit up the side. Personally, Nicole thought, she wouldn't be caught dead wearing it. Designed by a top fashion designer or not, this dress was ugly with a capital U. It seemed the designer was relying on showing skin instead of talent with an intended attempt to get a man's attention. She made a mental note to tell her manager not to accept any more assignments from this designer. Being able to choose assignments was one of the benefits to being one of the country's top models. She gave the photographer a posed, fierce smile, with the light catching her high cheekbones, her blue eyes gleaming.

"Great!" the photographer said sharply. "Go change and make it quick."

Without a word, Nicole changed into the next dress, an ugly blue sheath. Before the afternoon was over, she went through three more dresses. As she posed, she was hiding the boredom she felt. All she could think was: Home, tomorrow, I'll be home. Just one more runway show to go and she could hit the plane. She had her flight booked to leave a few hours after the show and arrive at home late the next day.

Runway shows were hectic, fast and furious. She changed into outfit after outfit not caring who was there or who saw her, man or woman. She dressed, walked, and dressed again. There was no time for modesty, no time for a sip of water, and no time to breathe.

She wanted to get out of the business, but kept that thought to herself remembering the old saying: be careful what you wish for.

Following the show's finale, she pulled on her usual jeans and white T-shirt. As things began to wind down and everyone made their plans for after the show she turned down offers from the other models and stylists crowded in the dressing area. The offers included drinks, parties, drugs, and even some offers just to go out for dinner.

"You all know how much I want to get home," she said, then laughed with her usual good nature. "So I'll skip the parties and dinner. Of course, I'll definitely skip the drinks and drugs. You know they're against my beliefs."

By that point, some male admirers had come in with their own sets of offers. She turned these down as well. She liked most of the women she worked with. Most of them were decent, hard-working, and intelligent. Of course, there were also the ones who used drugs or alcohol, and the ones who either used men, or let men use them. These types of women were found in every business.

Nicole tried not to judge these women, it was not her place. Instead, she would try to find ways to offer advice or the word of God when she could, but she had to be very careful. It would take just one time of pushing too hard or offering a wrong word to send them running away from God instead of towards Him. It was hard to be a devout Christian in her line of work, but that's what she was determined to be. Although she was ready to get out of modeling, she also believed there was something remaining for her to do. She felt the time was coming, but it was not there yet.

As she was gathering her things in a well-worn duffel bag,

one of the younger models came over to her with tears in her eyes. The young girl was barely eighteen, exotic looking with golden skin and cat-like green eyes.

"Nicole," she asked quietly, "can I talk to you?"

"Sure, Natalia. I can tell you're upset. What's the problem?" She took the girl's arm and led her to an out of the way sofa.

"I'm pregnant!" If there was such a thing as a whispered wail, this was it. "I'll have to have an abortion, and I know you don't believe in them, but what can I do?"

"First, are you sure? Have you taken a test?" Nicole put her arms around the girl's shoulder.

"I'm sure!" She sobbed. "I took the test."

"And is the father willing to be involved? Will he stand by you?" She reached over and grabbed some tissues.

"I don't know if he will or not, but I don't want to trap him." Natalia's sobs quieted without ceasing. "I have to abort it."

"Natalia, how would you feel if you gave someone very important to you a gift, one designed especially for them, and they refused it?" Nicole rubbed Natalia's shoulder.

"I'd be hurt and angry." Natalia managed to eke out an answer.

"What if the gift you gave her was alive, a puppy or a kitten, and they didn't just refuse it, they killed it right in front of you?" She kept rubbing, her voice low and non-judgmental.

"I'd be devastated." Natalia looked up.

"That's exactly what you want to do with a gift from God," Nicole said quietly. "So why don't we look at some other options. You said the baby's father might be willing to help, so first, if I were you I'd find out what he's willing to do. Marriage? Child support? Would he want to be a part of this child's life? You need to talk to him, regardless of what he says."

Nicole rose and got some cold water for Natalia before continuing. "And your parents, would they help you?"

"They'd be ashamed of me," Natalia admitted.

3

"But would they help you?" Nicole persisted.

"Yes, I think they would." Natalia gave a hint of a smile.

"So step two is talking to your parents." Nicole sat down again and stroked the young woman's hair. "And the next thing is to find a way to earn a living for when you stop modeling. Do you have any skills or education?"

"I have a few semesters of college," Natalia said. "I was studying Medical Transcription. I even had good grades."

"Do you see all the options you have?" Nicole asked. "Now my next question, are you a Christian?"

"Not really, I have been to church but I never joined." Natalia looked at Nicole. "Does it really matter?"

"More than anything, ever." Nicole looked her in the eye and said, "If you've been attending church for any length of time you have heard how Jesus came to earth to save sinners, and that he died, was buried and rose again on the third day for us. He offers salvation as a free gift to those who will simply ask him for it. He paid for our sins if we accept him. Do you accept Jesus Christ as your Lord and Savior?"

"Well, yes," Natalia murmured.

"Will you come to church with me when you get back to Southern California?" Nicole smiled.

"Yes." Natalia's face expressed a genuine smile.

Nicole took the girl's hand and said a short prayer for her.

"Are you all right for now? I have to either catch my plane or change my reservation." Nicole stood up. "Call me anytime, okay Sweetie? If you don't get back home soon, find a pastor here and talk to him." She hugged Natalia.

Nicole walked out to the already waiting cab and headed for the airport. It was a quiet flight home. She arrived at her home in Orange County, California in the late afternoon. She sat down with her family, her growing family, and relaxed for a while. She talked and ate a bite with her older brother David and his wife Emily, who was still nursing their baby, Pete. They were soon joined by Mae, Emily's mother, who suffered from senile dementia and her nurse, Julia, who got some iced tea for herself and Mae.

"Sister," Mae said to Nicole, her pale blue eyes filled with sympathy, "you gotta get out of this house once in a while. You can't just sit around here all day long."

"Mae, I just got home. I was gone for two weeks." Nicole smiled.

Mae was good-natured, even if she lived in a different world. "That's you young people, always flitting around."

Nicole shook her head with a small smile, sometimes you just couldn't win with Mae.

David had to go to work for a late meeting in his law office while Emily went upstairs for a short nap with Pete. Julia took Mae back upstairs, leaving Nicole alone in the gleaming kitchen, so she decided to go outside for a while. She ran upstairs to get her bathing suit and a towel, and exchanged her shoes for some riding boots.

She walked down the hill to the small barn and greeted all three horses, then saddled Burgie, her bay gelding. She rode him into the arena, working the arena gate while mounted on Burgie's back. She side-stepped him up to the gate, reached down to open it, and side-stepped him out again, then she rode through and side-stepped him over to close the gate.

The arena was fairly large, making it big enough to set up any of the gymkhana events. David kept the ground well-groomed to ensure good footing. The arena fences were solid and freshly painted, and best of all, someone had left the barrels set up. She carefully warmed up Burgie before turning him to face the barrels from the end of the arena. She gave him a quick nudge in his side, made a click of her tongue, and they set off. Burgie knew barrels really well, and enjoyed his run. He was fast, and had terrific turns around the cloverleaf pattern. As they finished the ride, Burgie slid to a stop at the arena fence, tossed his head and pranced.

Nicole knew he wanted to run again but she was tired from her trip, so she took Burgie over and unsaddled him. She hosed him off and snapped his halter to the hot walker.

She cleaned the stalls, put up her tack and straightened up the tack room, using it to change into her bathing suit. It was weird to be wearing a bathing suit with her boots, but she did. She went out wearing the suit and turned off the hot walker. After unsnapping Burgie's halter from the machine she pulled his halter off and let him find his own way into his stall. She closed his stall door, gathered her jeans and T-shirt, and headed across the lawn for the pool.

The pool was longer and thinner than most. It was designed more for laps than recreation. There was a fence around the pool, tall and sturdy enough to keep kids and Mae out. There were hedges outside the fence, and a few taller trees spaced here and there. Nicole put her clothes on a lounge chair, pulled off her boots, and jumped in.

She swam laps for about half an hour, then got out and soaked in the hot tub for a few minutes. Finally she stretched out on a lounge chair and took a nap. She woke up soon and realized she'd better get back inside. She sighed, a model could not afford a tan or tan lines. She watched TV for a while, and then went up to bed around 9 PM.

Nicole woke up early and just laid there for a moment, feeling lazy and reflecting on her life. She knew she had it remarkably easy. Her career as one of the world's top models was at its peak, and she already had plans in place for a new career that was based on more than her looks. She planned to open a gym for women who were what the rest of the world called imperfect.

Most of the women she wanted to help were overweight by today's standards. They were women who felt insecure or lacked self-confidence. She had a requirement for women who wanted to join her gym because of their weight: they had to be at least 50 pounds overweight. Her goal was to help them become healthy and gain confidence, not to lose weight. She felt so strongly about this because she had a friend who had died from an eating disorder while trying to be what the world called perfect.

Nicole had covered all the bases. She had a crew of make-up people and hairdressers on hand to give them makeovers. Dietitians and doctors were also on call to make sure the women were healthy. She planned to give them monthly photo sessions in order to show any improvement and to help them see the genuine beauty they had inside, the way she saw them. Her favorite photographer, Hans, would shoot the pictures. He had shot the world's top models, and knew how to bring out the best in a subject. She had counselors who would meet with anyone who wanted to build their self-esteem. She also had two pastors available for those who needed or desired spiritual counseling.

Nicole knew she was blessed, but she also knew she was more than a pretty face and wanted to help women learn how to get the most out of their lives.

Her world was not perfect, however. She thought of her brother David who had gotten married just over a year ago. Nicole loved her new sister-in-law, Emily, and her brand new nephew, Pete. She was envious of them and their love and joy in each other, and the baby. Their happiness brought one thing home to her, she was tired of her single state, and she hated being judged and pursued by men who only saw her face, her body, or her bank account, sometimes all three. She wanted to find someone who loved her for herself and marry him. Still, she couldn't think of a real problem in her life. She put everything in the hands of God. She smiled to herself and said a prayer of thanks before getting out of bed.

Since it was her turn to care for the horses, she pulled on her sweats, and wandered out to the barn to feed the horses and clean the stalls. She walked over to her horse, Burgie, a half-quarter horse half-Arab gelding and gave him a good morning rub, stroking his velvet nose, before turning him out into the arena. She moved on to her brother's horse, Target, a heavily muscled black quarter horse, giving him the same greeting before turning him out. Finally, she gave the same treatment to Emily's sorrel quarter horse gelding, Raider. She gave each horse a few bites of a carrot before letting them run. She went from stall to stall, putting their hay in the feeders, and adding their portions of grain and vitamins. She checked the automatic waterers in each stall and then when all of this was done she got a wheelbarrow and pitchfork and mucked each stall, laughing to herself as she thought of how her fans probably envied her glamorous life. Well, they did have the horses, she mused. That was glamour and luxury to most people, even with shoveling the manure.

She caught all three horses easily by just opening their stall doors and letting them walk in. They were hungry for their hay.

She scraped her boots off before she walked back up the hill to the house. She changed her boots for sneakers and made her way downstairs to the gym for a workout. She grunted her way through her daily routine, which included free weights and aerobics. Sometimes she would put in a workout video and do that routine. Today, she skipped that and just took a quick swim. She went back upstairs to her room, laying out her clothes for the day before taking her shower and washing her hair. She pulled on her customary jeans and a soft blue T-shirt. Finally she was ready to face her day. She grabbed her keys and headed downstairs.

Everything was much easier, she smiled thinking to herself, since her brother had expanded the house. He had built a master suite for himself and Emily, a room for the baby, and a small suite for Emily's mother, Mae, and her nurse, Julia. They had been living in Emily's old house, but having them here was so much better. He had also added the gym downstairs.

Nicole stopped in the cheery kitchen for a bite of breakfast. She sat down at the large round kitchen table and spoke to Julia and Mae. Julia was a sweet, still attractive woman in her early sixties. She was a retired RN, with the patience and firmness needed to care for Mae. Emily's mother could be quite a handful, loving and full of fun, but a handful.

Mae was lively and friendly, but really out of touch with reality. She once came home from a day in a local zoo and told Nicole that she'd gone to Russia. Nicole listened with patient amusement as Mae gave a detailed description of the "Russian" zoo. Julia was a retired RN who had lived next door. She was a widow who had been left with a large house and five acres of land. David bought the land, not the house, and offered Julia a place to live along with a part-time job. She was a real godsend. Julia quickly became part of the family, and life was much easier for David and Emily, especially with the new baby.

From what Julia told Nicole as she sat down to a glass of orange juice and a plate of fluffy scrambled eggs, Mae was having one of her good days. She recognized Emily and Pete. In fact, Julia seemed to think the baby, six-month-old Pete, had done quite a bit to stem Mae's senile dementia.

Nikki finished her eggs and put her plate into the dishwasher. She grabbed her travel mug, some bottled water and an energy bar, and jumped into her car. She had a modeling assignment that day and wanted to leave herself plenty of time for hair and make-up. This assignment was for a new client, someone she had never even heard of, which was unusual. She had gotten the location and time from her agent, Melinda, who said she'd meet her there, since she didn't know anything about the client either. Halfway there, Melinda called and said she was sick. She sounded terrible. She offered to send an assistant but Nicole declined the offer, telling her to stay home and take care of herself.

She was shocked when she arrived at the address, since it was in a rundown part of town and the building fit right in with its surroundings. The brick building was old and tacky. Several bricks were missing and it was covered with vulgar graffiti and gang symbols. One of the windows was broken. The door squeaked when she opened it, and there were dust motes floating in the air.

Another blow to the glamorous life of a model, she thought. In truth she often worked in less than ideal conditions, but this? With the dirt and trash scattered all over the floor, the moldy smell, and no furnishings, this was ridiculous!

There was a bare minimum of equipment and supplies for the photo shoot. Along one wall there was a rack of bathing suits. A plain white backdrop stood at the end of the room with some lights and a camera on a tripod facing it. On the other wall there was a make-up table covered with cosmetics, brushes, combs and a hot iron for her hair. Next to it was another table with some pastries and a pot of coffee with some plates and cups.

Her make-up and hair people, Ivan and Lacey, walked in just after she did, both looking around at the room with distaste. Hans, who was acting as her stylist for this shoot, and not as the photographer, was not far behind.

The photographer was not there yet. Nicole shrugged and sat patiently while her hair and make-up was being done. She chatted casually with Hans and the hairdresser, Ivan, and Lacey who did her make-up. Lacey had pictures of her new baby with her, a tiny daughter with a jaunty pink headband on blonde curly hair and an adorable grin, both of which matched her mother's features.

"Maybe she'll grow up to marry my nephew Pete," Nikki quipped, smiling at the baby. She brought out a picture of Pete, also grinning but sans pink headband, and with curly brown hair. She handed it over to Lacey.

As expected, Lacey grinned at the photo and told Nicole how cute he was.

She dressed in the wardrobe provided for the shoot, skimpy and not very attractive swimwear. She noticed a young man watching her from across the room, who was wearing worn jeans and a red T-shirt. She assumed he was either the photographer or his assistant. He walked over to her.

"Hi, I'm Adam," he said, then smiled and held out his hand

and introduced himself. "Mr. Scarleni's assistant. He just called me and asked me to apologize for him. He is running late and should be here in about fifteen minutes. He suggested you all have some coffee and pastries."

"No, thanks. I brought my own coffee." Nicole smiled at him, but she was surprised at the flash of irritation that crossed his face.

Still, Adam seemed like a nice young man. He was in his mid-twenties, lanky and handsome. His wavy brown hair fell into his eyes. He reached out and took Nicole's hand in a seemingly friendly manner, but he held it just a bit too long. His brown eyes seemed intense as they stared into hers. He completely ignored the rest of the crew and focused on Nicole. Something about him disturbed her but she shook it off.

It was rare for the photographer to be late, but Nicole was a pro and sat quietly on a rickety chair, sipping her travel mug of coffee until she heard a noise behind her. It was a thud, followed by another. Just as she turned her head to see what made the noise, she thought she smelled a hint of smoke. Before she could react, she felt a sharp pain and the world exploded.

Chapter Two

"These things I have spoken unto you, that in me ye might have peace. In this world ye shall have tribulation: But be ye of good cheer; I have overcome the world."
(John 16:33)

David would never forget receiving that terrible phone call. He was in London at the time, working with a client who was having a dispute with a designer over her contract. He got the call from the police saying that Nicole was in the hospital, that she had been attacked and was not expected to live. His heart felt squeezed in his chest. He explained hastily to his client and the designer that there was an emergency back in LA. He called his mother, Bonnie, to let her know what had happened although he didn't have very many details. She told him she would fly out right away.

David was panicked on the flight, barely able to stay in his seat, and not at all able to relax.

"You seem upset, sir, is there anything I can do for you?" a flight attendant said when she came over to see what was wrong.

"I'm terrified. My sister was attacked, I don't know the details." Because he was so upset, he told the flight attendant what was going on. "They said they didn't expect her to live."

"What's her name?" The flight attendant said with genuine sympathy, "I'll say a prayer for her."

"Thank you," David replied. "Her name's Nicole, Nikki Silver."

When the flight attendant gasped, he added, "Please don't tell anyone she's hurt, until I know more I don't want it to get into the press."

"I understand. I was almost afraid to walk over and talk to

you," she told him. "I wondered if you were some kind of lunatic. Now I wish that's all that was bothering you. I'll try to see if I can clear your flight plans to get you there as fast as possible. Where are you flying to?"

"John Wayne." David managed a smile then said, "Thanks for helping me. They said I had to fly standby from New York to LAX and again into John Wayne."

"I'll do what I can," she promised as she patted his shoulder and moved on to help another passenger. "We try very hard to accommodate people if there's an emergency in the family."

The flight seemed endless, and he had to change planes in New York. There he had a short layover before he could get on another flight, but he could tell the flight attendant had cleared the way for him. For the last short leg of his journey his layover was again very brief. Still, the trip seemed endless. All he could do was pray and keep praying that Nicole would be alright. He just didn't know how he could handle it if she didn't survive.

He didn't have very much information about what had happened, only that she was very seriously hurt in an attack by some mad man, and was now in the hospital. He tried calling her agent but he couldn't get ahold of her. He tried calling Emily, but didn't reach her either. No one seemed to be answering their cell phones. He could only guess that cell phones weren't allowed in that part of the hospital. What he didn't know was that the police had not yet been able to contact Emily simply because she had been shopping without her cell phone, and then had gone out to the barn to take care of the horses. Julia had taken a message but then Mae started getting agitated and Julia had her hands full.

Since their mother was in Florida, she was much closer to Nicole than David was in Paris. She arrived at John Wayne Airport sooner than David did. She rented a car and left her bags in the trunk, heading straight for the hospital in Mission Viejo. She got to the hospital to see Nicole long before David did. She was a strong woman who had seen a lot in her life but she was still in a state of panic. She was the one who finally reached Emily. Soon Emily joined her at the hospital and they prayed together. Emily called her pastor who came immediately and prayed with them and just sat and tried to comfort them.

Nicole was in a sterile environment and only medical staff was allowed in her room, so Bonnie and Emily paced the halls until they almost wore a hole in the linoleum. By the time David arrived they had begun to settle down, one or the other sitting for a few moments, and then popping up to pace again. David's mom ran to hug him as tears streamed down her face. She was terrified at the thought that she would lose Nicole, but she figured every minute that Nicole was being treated was one more sign that she would be okay.

Emily stood to one side and waited while David hugged his mother before she walked over to him. She loved Nicole too, but she knew that a parent's love for her child was overwhelming. When David was ready, he turned to hug and kiss her. He was shaking and there were tears in his eyes, but he drew on Emily's love and strength. It was several moments before he turned to Pastor Mark and thanked him for being there. They said a prayer as a group before one of the doctors came out to talk to them.

"Hi, I'm Dr. Wilson, and I'm taking care of Nicole," he said. "The good news is it looks like Nicole's chances of survival are fairly good. If we can keep her from getting an infection, we have every hope she'll make a recovery. She is in a coma now, but that can be a good thing, it will keep her from feeling some of the pain from her injuries. Burn treatment is very painful. Also, there are some complications and things that we can't correct. We cannot stop her from being scarred. I understand that she's a high fashion model and I'm sorry, but I believe this will end her career."

"Hi Dr. Wilson, I'm David Silvan, this is my mother, Bonnie Silvan, and my wife, Emily. The little guy in the stroller is my son, Pete. We're most concerned about Nicole's survival. Her looks are not that important, her life is. We will do everything, of course, that we can do to help her heal. And we'll be praying for her constantly. What other issues are you worried about right now?"

"I don't know if you heard about what happened to her," the doctor said, "but Nicole was attacked, beaten, and raped, then left to die in a burning building."

He paused as Bonnie gasped, tears streaming down her face.

He continued, "So aside from healing and scars, there is a possibility that she was left emotionally scarred, or with a sexually transmitted disease, or even made pregnant by the attack."

"We can treat her emotionally, and test her for the diseases, but it's too soon to tell if there's a possible pregnancy." The doctor continued, "Unless she was pregnant already?"

He made it a question. As they all shook their heads, he continued once more. "I thought not. Her injuries seemed to indicate that she was a virgin. I would recommend using a morning after pill to prevent pregnancy. I'm sure she would not want to become pregnant by a rapist and a murderer."

"Who was murdered?" David asked, chills running down his spine. "We haven't heard many details yet."

"As I understand it, three people she worked with died in the fire," the doctor replied. "Lacey Knolls, Hans Weston, and Ivan Hudsen."

At this news, Emily, who knew Nicole's co-workers, was overcome. Her legs buckled and she had to sit down. Tears were streaming down her face.

"Nicole has given me the power of attorney in case of an emergency, we set it up a long time ago. I know she doesn't believe in the morning after pill, so I have to say no to any use of the pill." David was firm. "If she's pregnant, there's a reason. If I'm wrong, she'll have to wake up and tell me so."

"One of you can go in for a few minutes if you wear a gown, mask and gloves." The doctor motioned to a nurse who came over. "Then you can switch, but only two of you, no more than five minutes each."

The nurse helped Bonnie put on the gown and gloves, and showed her a chair at Nicole's bedside.

When her time was up, David took his position by Nicole's bedside. Emily and Bonnie knew they were in for a long vigil. They could sit there for days, waiting for Nicole to wake up or go home. They decided to leave.

Bonnie got to the house, and instantly Julia insisted on carrying her bags upstairs to a room she had prepared in advance. Bonnie pulled a nightgown out of her luggage, took a quick shower and went to bed, exhausted but unable to sleep.

Nicole was in a coma for nearly two weeks. Then she started waking up, at first only for a few moments at a time. She woke up several times over the next days and weeks in pain, intense pain. Waking to strange surroundings with a constant beeping sound in the background, she knew she was in a hospital. Doctors and nurses were constantly treating her, their faces covered by masks, and wearing sterile gowns. She had an IV in both arms. She woke up extremely thirsty and hungry.

Every time she slipped back into sleep she seemed to forget where she was, and each time she awoke she faced the horror of not knowing what had happened to her. Gradually, she became more aware of herself, her surroundings, and her circumstances. She realized she was in a hospital bed surrounded by glass walls and curtains. There were the constant IVs and monitors, of course, and nurses constantly coming in and out of the room. She realized she was in a hospital, probably in ICU or a burn unit, judging by the IVs sticking out of her arms. She was more than aware of the painful treatments.

She later learned the doctors had used both chemical and autolytic debridement, and in some areas where the burns were less severe they had already begun skin grafts. Gradually, as the days went on, she became aware that the doctors and nurses had stopped wearing masks while around her. They moved her to another room. She didn't know it at the time, but she had moved from the burn unit to ICU. After arriving there she was aware that she had visitors.

Sometimes her brother and Emily would sit beside her while at other times her mother was there, or her friends, Kate and Laura. Of course, her pastor, Mark, and his wife, Rachel, frequently visited in order to chat, pray, and read the Bible. Although she was aware of their coming and going, she was not strong enough or aware enough to respond to them, except with an occasional moan or a blink of the eye. At times she would manage to give a gentle squeeze to the hand holding her hand.

For the most part her visitors sat in an uncomfortable chair, staring at the blank beige walls, or watching whatever was showing on the wall-mounted TV screen. They watched nurses and lab techs come and go, taking blood samples, changing IVs, and making notes on a small computer in the corner of the room. Once in a while a doctor checked in and quickly left.

For weeks, any efforts she made to speak were met by quiet shushings, "Just relax Nicole, I know you're hurting and probably in a great deal of pain, but for now just try to relax, rest and heal," her brother softly told her.

For weeks it seemed as if that was all she heard. So that's what she did, she waited, rested and healed.

"What happened?" she moaned one day when she woke more fully.

"Thank God, you're awake." David gently took her hand, he paused for a moment swallowing hard before he continued. "Don't you remember what happened?"

Nicole's voice was scratchy and weak but she managed a faint, "No."

"You were injured in a fire." David kept her hand in his, wishing he could avoid telling her what he knew she had to hear. "The building where your photo shoot was being held burned down."

"How? Why?" She swallowed hard, David handed her a cup of water with a straw.

"I checked with your doctors, you can have a sip of water, just a little sip, now," he warned her. "Take it easy."

She sipped before continuing, "What about the others? What about Ivan, Lacey and Hans, my friends who do my hair and make-up? My stylist? Even Adam, the photographer's assistant. Are they okay? Please, David, please tell me, tell me they're okay."

"I'm sorry, Nick," David said softly grasping her hand, "more than I can say, but you were the only survivor."

"Dead? All of them?" Tears formed in her eyes. "Hans, Ivan and Lacey? They were all my friends. Lacey's baby is only three months old."

She broke into uncontrollable sobs.

"I know, Nick, I know." David could only stand there, patting her hand gently while she cried. Luckily, Pastor Mark and Rachel came in at that exact moment.

When he saw her distress, Pastor Mark put his hands on Nicole's shoulders. Rachel put a hand on her hair. While they stood there touching Nicole, they prayed.

"Heavenly Father, we pray for our sister Nicole. Father God, she has been so badly injured, grant her a miracle and help her heal. Send your love and blessings to her. Bless also the families and loved ones of those who were killed in this terrible incident. Father God, let their souls rest in your arms and send your heavenly comfort to their loved ones and families, Lord. Comfort Nicole, Father God, and give her peace. Show her a way to turn this tragedy into a triumph, for I know you have a purpose for her. Show her that purpose. Comfort her and bring her healing and peace, in Jesus' name. Amen."

Pastor Mark and Rachel sat and talked to Nicole for a long time and did not leave until her tears and sobs quieted.

David said gently, "We've prayed for their families, Nicole. Also, Emily and I have done whatever we can do to help them, but it's not enough. They're gone and their families are devastated. We set up scholarships for their children. It's not just you, you know, Nicole. Emily knew them and loved them, too. Remember how Hans helped her gain confidence? He shot hundreds of photos of her looking beautiful, so that finally she was able to see what we saw. We're all really grief stricken and scared. There's another thing you have to be aware of, this was no accident. The fire was deliberately set. Until we catch whoever did this, your life may be in danger."

"We're also puzzled," Emily added. "The police can't figure out what happened, or why."

"The police want to talk to you when you're able." David said, "They seem to think you were the target, that you were the reason the fire was set."

"Oh my God!" Nikki covered her eyes, it was several minutes before she could talk. "Who would do something like that? Why?"

"The police are investigating, of course, but we don't know." David held her hand gently.

"How long has it been?" she asked quietly.

"About five weeks," David said softly. "You've been burned, mainly second degree, but some third, and you also suffered a concussion. You were in a coma for about two weeks and..."

David paused to collect himself, going to a new subject to gain time, "Mom is here, she's staying at the house. She's having quite a time getting along with Mae, or not getting along, depending on how aware Mae is from day to day."

David grinned then continued, "She'll be here soon, Mom, not Mae. It's been hard on her, on all of us. We thought... well, you know what we thought, but God is good and you are healing. You've had several surgeries and skin grafts already. And Nick, I think you should know... well, a couple of things."

"What is it David?" she asked quietly, too shaken by the loss of her friends to be worried about anything, or so she thought.

"First," but just as he started to talk, Pastor Brad, from the church Emily had attended before she married David, came into the room. He still considered himself a minister for the family, and they did too.

"Hi, Pastor." Emily smiled at him. "It's good to see you."

"Hi, Nicole," Pastor Brad said. "I know Pastor Mark has been doing a great job of praying for you, but I'd like to put in my two cents worth and pray for you too."

"I'd appreciate that." Nicole smiled. "I need all the help I can get."

Pastor Brad prayed over Nicole.

After he finished, David told Pastor Brad, "This is a good time for your visit, I was telling Nicole some things about her injuries, and well…"

He turned to Nicole and said, "Honey, they did a pregnancy test on you, to make sure none of the treatments would hurt the baby if, well, you were pregnant, if you are it's too soon to tell."

"David, I can't be." She almost sat up but her brother held her down. "I know it's weird at my age but I've never…" She turned to Pastor Brad. "I haven't."

"I believe you," he said calmly. "I know you."

"Nick, we know you were raped rather violently. There was massive bruising and tearing." David hesitated then continued, "If you did get pregnant with all of that trauma, it would be amazing."

"It would be a miracle if you didn't lose the fetus." He paused again. "There was some discussion about giving you a morning after pill, but I had power of attorney for medical decisions. Remember when we set that up?"

At her nod, he continued, "So I was acting as your guardian while you were unable to make decisions and I know how you feel about abortion, even morning after pills. I thought it should be your decision."

"You're right. I would feel terrible if I had that decision taken away from me." She looked up at David. "How long has it been since I was tested?"

"About ten days," he explained to her, hesitating just a bit. "They said... um."

"Men!" Emily jumped in. "They said it would help them if they knew when your next period was due."

Nicole tried to calculate. "I was due for it to start on the 17th, give or take, so that would be about two weeks after the attack."

"I'll tell the nurse," David said and left the room.

Soon a nurse came and took some blood. David returned to the room.

He stood and paced, his hands in his pockets now, wondering how much pain he would have to inflict on a sister he loved so much. "Also, I know this isn't a priority for you, but let's face it: your career is over. You'll have some scars, a lot of scars."

David walked over to hold her hand. "Do you want me to get a mirror so you can see your face?"

"Not yet, David, okay? I'm just not ready." She managed a weak smile.

"At least you still have your beautiful hair," David managed. "One side of your hair had to be cut short, but it's growing back."

"Woo hoo!" she managed to quip. Then she met David's eyes and continued softly, "I'll be okay, you know. I had a retirement plan worked out. I was tired of being judged only by my looks, and I never wanted to stretch my modeling into an acting career like some models do. So I have the plans for my gym. I'm set pretty well financially, too. I've got great medical insurance, plus extra insurance on my face, and I've invested my earnings pretty well, thanks to you."

She sighed, with some resignation. "It'll work out. What else?"

"Well, there is one more thing: You might hear a report on TV. They're saying you died in the fire."

There was a long pause.

"Nikki Silver did die in the fire." She held up her chin as she said, "Nicole Silvan is recovering. She's a survivor."

A nurse came in and said, "I have the results of her pregnancy test. So do you want to have some privacy for this?"

"No, my friends and family can hear the results." Nicole sipped more water.

With Pastor Brad holding one hand and David holding the other, they looked to the nurse.

"You are pregnant. I can send for an OB/GYN to come and discuss your pregnancy with you later today, if you'd like," she said calmly.

Then she turned to David, "I think she's had enough for now. Let her rest and you can come back later."

She shooed the trio out of the room at about the same time Nicole's mother arrived. She burst into the room, full of energy and concern. Her blue eyes flashed as she took in Nicole's condition. She had something for Nicole, she brought some of her nightgowns, and even some shorts and T-shirts. Changing into a real nightgown made Nicole feel as if the end was in sight, she was getting well, it was a real morale booster. After a short visit, Bonnie left too, promising to come back later with David.

After her mother left, Nicole sighed in relief. She wept with the emotions she had suppressed in front of her family, and then drifted off to sleep.

Later that day she met with Dr. Sullivan, the chief resident OB/GYN. They chatted briefly, and the doctor ran some tests. She told Nicole they had time to decide on how to handle the pregnancy, along with what treatment and care she would need. She promised to check on Nicole the next day, and then she left.

The next day she got a pleasant surprise, Jello! Cherry Jello! After so long of not eating anything except what came from a feeding tube, IVs and occasional sips of water, it was heaven. She could only eat a few spoonfuls but she savored every bite.

The OB/GYN came in. This time Nicole was aware enough to notice her name tag, Dr. Wendy Sullivan. She met the doctor's wide smile and said, "Hi, I'm Nicole Silvan, glad to meet you."

Doctor Sullivan shook her hand. "I thought you were a little um, shell-shocked when we met yesterday."

There was warmth and humor in her soft brown eyes. "It's no wonder. You've had quite a shock."

"Several of them," Nicole agreed, still smiling.

The doctor couldn't know it was her professional smile.

"I have to run, but for now, I have one question. At this point do you intend to go through with the pregnancy?" she asked.

"Of course," Nicole nodded. "Why not?"

"Why not indeed?" Dr. Sullivan looked at her pager and quickly left.

Behind her, Nicole laid there praying for strength and guidance, and confidence in her decision.

Chapter Three

"Is any sick among you? Let him call for the elders of the church; and let them pray over him, anointing him with oil in the name of the Lord: And the prayer of faith shall save the sick, and the Lord shall raise him up; if he have committed sins; they shall be forgiven him."
(James 5:14-15)

Later in the day, two police detectives came in to talk to Nicole. The older detective was a middle-aged woman with gray hair, brown eyes, a tough face and a tender manner. She was dressed in tailored charcoal gray slacks with a trim white shirt and dark blue blazer. She sat beside Nicole and did most of the talking. Her partner was a great looking man of about thirty with green eyes and wavy brown hair. He sat further away. He crossed his legs, balancing his notebook on his jeans and took notes. He listened, only interjecting with a few questions.

"Hi, I'm Detective Mollney, and this is my partner, Detective Reynolds. I'm very sorry about your injuries, and the loss of your friends." She paused. "Can we turn down the TV? Or off?"

She reached for the remote even as she asked.

"Off would be fine," Nicole answered.

"What can you tell us about what happened to you?" Detective Mollney continued, now that the TV was off.

"I don't remember very much about that day," Nicole admitted slowly. "I'll admit, a small part of me is glad I don't remember. What woman would want to remember being raped and brutalized, and having her good friends murdered? What little I can remember is very painful and confused. Of course, I also want to help you catch whoever is responsible for this, so I am trying to remember anything that can help."

Nicole paused and looked at Detective Mollney. "It's not just about my injuries and the loss of my career. They are not really the most important things. He killed three of my friends."

Her breath hitched. "They were very good people."

There was a long pause before she continued, "I was tired that day, I just came back from a show in Australia the day before. Maybe I wasn't alert or cautious enough. All I remember is that I received an assignment to go to a photo shoot for a new client. I'd never heard of the designer before; I know most of the fashion designers in the area, but I was not really suspicious. I went to the address I was given. The neighborhood was run down and the building was dirty and in disrepair."

She paused and shook her head. "I really should have been more suspicious."

"Why weren't you suspicious?" Detective Reynolds asked. "Why didn't you just leave?"

"I was given the assignment by my agent and I didn't want to let her down. I wanted to be professional. Word gets out when a model fails to show up for an assignment, or when she walks out. The next thing you know, you can't get booked for anything, even a fashion show at the mall," she explained, sipping her soft drink before adding with a small, tight grin, "And of course, I didn't want to be a big wuss."

She grinned. "I mean, if I left, all those people would be out their money, the three who died all depended on me for their income. I didn't want to let them down."

Her smile faded. "Now, I wish I had."

"I had my hair and make-up done before the photographer arrived, in fact, his assistant came over and said he would be there in about fifteen minutes. That was very unusual, the photogs are usually not only on time, but they love accusing everyone else of being late and holding up a shoot. Most of them go off on rants about how time is money. The others on my team got some coffee and pastries the photog's assistant had put out but I already had my own blend of coffee in my own mug, and I avoid pastries, for my figure. Part of the job. I just sat there and waited for the photographer to arrive."

"What was the photographer's name?" Detective Mollney asked.

"I'm sorry, I don't remember. My agent can tell you." She smiled as a nurse brought her a cup of coffee, even though she already had a soft drink. "Now that I'm allowed to drink, they hardly let me finish one before bringing another. Would either of you like some coffee or a soda?"

Both detectives declined.

"And his assistant's name?" Detective Mollney asked, returning to her questions.

"I remember that he introduced himself as Adam, I didn't get a last name," she said sadly. "He was good looking and seemed really nice."

"Can you describe him?" She was prodded.

"Yes, he was young. Brown hair and eyes, a bit swarthy, great smile, well-built but slender, about 5'10" and I'd say about mid-twenties."

"How do you remember so many details of his description? And how sure of it are you?" Detective Mollney asked, surprised.

"My job is about descriptions and appearances." She paused. "Also I thought he would do great as a model."

"Anything else?" Detective Mollney asked. "What else can you tell us about that day?"

"I thought I heard a noise, a kind of thud, and I smelled what I thought was smoke. I turned my head to see what was up, and felt... well, it felt like the world exploded."

"How did you get the assignment?" Detective Mollney asked.

"My manager, Melinda Jacobson from All Star Modeling, emailed it to me."

"Was that the way you usually got your assignments?" the detective asked.

"No, but it's not unheard of." Nicole grinned. "Usually Melinda phones me and we chat about anything and everything. She only uses email when she's too busy to talk."

"Was there anything else that seemed unusual about the assignment?" she prodded.

"Yes." She paused. "Usually when I go to a new client, one neither Melinda nor I knew, she would go too or send an assistant as a sort of back-up."

"Why didn't she go this time?" the younger detective, Detective Reynolds, asked.

"Let me think. She called and said she was ill, so I told her to stay home and take care of herself." Nicole sighed. "Thank God she wasn't there."

"How did Melinda sound when you spoke to her on the phone?" Detective Reynolds asked quietly. "Did she sound ill? Or upset?"

"She sounded ill, kind of choked up." Nicole paused, thinking. "Why?"

"I'm very sorry to tell you that Melinda Jacobson was found dead in her apartment," he said quietly. Pausing, he added, "Her throat was slit. She was murdered the same day as the fire."

"Oh my God!" Nicole broke down sobbing. "What's happening?"

"We don't know," the female detective spoke quietly. "We're investigating of course, but so far, we just don't know."

The officers waited until she came under some control.

"Have you been getting stalked, obsessed fans, death threats, anything like that?" Detective Mollney asked. "Think back several months. Is there anything that stands out? That seems suspicious in hindsight?"

"There's always someone, some fan who thinks I love him, or that he loves me. Someone who thinks I'm a slut because I'm a model. It's part of being, well, famous. We keep a file with the details. Melinda has it stored on her computer," Nicole told her.

"Just in case."

"Melinda's office was broken into and her computer was stolen," the detective said.

"David has a back-up copy in his office, I don't think anyone knows about it. Plus he keeps all the original notes, letters or whatever," Nicole said, adding in desperation as a new thought hit her. "Please, he and Emily may need protection from this... this monster."

"We'll check with David and get the files. Also, we'll make sure he's safe," Detective Mollney said.

She pulled out her cell phone. "I need more protection to cover Nicole's family. Yes. Right away."

She looked over at Nicole. "We have protection on you and your family. You may not see them, but they'll be there."

They questioned her for another half-hour or so before they left. As soon as they were gone, she grieved and prayed for Melinda.

The next day Pastor Mark and Rachel came to visit and pray with her.

"I have to ask, Nikki, what are you going to do about the baby?" Rachel asked.

She put her hand over her face, fighting tears. "Rachel, Pastor, you know I don't believe in abortion, but I'll admit I thought and prayed about it. I just cannot bring myself to do it. I can't commit murder. Then I considered adoption but as I thought about it, I began to feel love for this baby. He or she is innocent. Actually, considering what I went through, what he went through, this baby is a miracle, a gift from God. I recently told a young model that her unexpected pregnancy was a gift from God. This one is the same, something wonderful coming out of evil and pain. How can I refuse to accept God's gift?"

Then she thought of something. "Pastor, has a young model named Natalia been in touch with you? I told her I'd bring her to church and introduce her to you but this happened. I don't even know if she thinks I forgot her, or if she knows I've been injured."

"David talked to her and told her what happened," Pastor Mark told her. "He brought her to church. She's going to marry her boyfriend next week."

"Thank God." Nicole whispered a prayer.

"Nicole, about your pregnancy, I know you are a good, loving woman," her pastor said. "I know you can give this child a good home, filled with joy and the love of God."

"Pastor, for a long time my life has been all about my looks. Not that my looks mattered that much to me, except as a, well, a business tool, you know that. Most people would think that I have to beat men off with a stick, that's the image they have of a model along with wild parties, jet setting and anorexia. Even before this happened I was getting tired of looking for the right man. I met a lot of men who seemed interested in me, but it was usually a false interest. Too many only saw this…" she made a circling gesture in front of her face, "or this body, or my bank account, even all three. Some wanted me to be sort of a pet or a trophy, and then some wanted to control me. They were just not right, not what I wanted at all."

She was firm as she said, "I wanted a man to really love me. I wanted a good Christian man; someone who could see the real me inside and not just the image or the bank account. I guess I don't have to worry about someone only being attracted to my looks anymore."

She shrugged.

"But now, how will anyone even look at me twice, to see the real me inside, with this face?" She admitted, "I finally got up the nerve to look in a mirror this morning and I'll admit it, I'm really shaken. I look horrible, and the scars will be there forever. Part of my hair is missing but it's growing back. There will be some improvement, with lots of care and countless plastic surgeries and time, but I will always have scars on my face and body. I know what's inside of me is more important than the shell but..."

"What a shock for you, for anyone." He prayed with her. "Father God, please be with Nicole as she goes through this trial. Help her heal. Bless her pregnancy and keep her baby safe. Help her find a good, loving father for this child and let it grow surrounded by love, in Jesus' name, Amen."

"Remember, it's in God's hands now." Rachel smiled, her lovely smile. "We just put it there."

"I have to admit, Pastor Mark, Rachel, my faith is a little shaky right now," Nicole said with a sad smile. "But I truly believe this baby, however he or she came into being, is a gift from God. This child will see the real me and feel my love. I may be on rocky ground in my faith right now, but it's still there."

Pastor Mark smiled at her. "I know you'll find a depth to your faith in the Lord that you didn't even know you had."

After the pastor and his wife left, Nicole started to feel worse. She felt warm and her skin felt clammy. Her chest felt tight as if it was being squeezed in a vise. She rang for the nurse only to find them already coming to her room.

"Relax, Nicole," the head nurse told her. "You're having some complications, but we're here and Doctor Wilson is coming. You're going to be fine."

"What's happening?" Nicole gasped. "I was feeling good and then I started feeling so weak."

"We're not sure, but we called the doctor as soon as we noticed the changes on your monitor," the nurse explained calmly. "He's coming any minute."

Behind her, Doctor Wilson strode up. "I'm here. Luckily I was visiting another patient."

The doctor looked over Nicole's charts and traces of her vitals.

He turned to the head nurse. "Book an O.R. stat. Tell them we have a pulmonary embolism."

He walked over to the head of Nicole's bed. "You've got a

pulmonary embolism; a blood clot in your lungs. We've been using medication to prevent this kind of clot but one has formed anyway. It can be treated with medication but I want to go in with a catheter and pull it out. This is done through a small incision, so it should heal quickly. Then we'll use medication to keep you from forming another one. You will be on it for months following your release from the hospital, and we will monitor your blood very closely. But for now, let's get this clot out."

He had her sign a consent form before they transferred her to a gurney and wheeled her into the surgical suite.

David rushed to the hospital as soon as he heard, only to be met there by his mother and Emily. Shortly after they arrived, Pastor Mark and Rachel joined them. They prayed and waited in a small waiting room designed for the families of ICU patients. Rachel poured everyone coffee.

"What makes this so frightening, for me at least, is that I was beginning to relax, feeling as if the worst was over," David said as he paced, "even if she's still in ICU."

"David, I spend a lot of time in this room with families," the pastor began, "and I know how much of a shock this is for you. I heard it was a pulmonary embolism, which is a serious setback, but it can be treated fairly easily. They caught it quickly because she is in ICU being closely monitored. The surgery they are doing on her is minimally invasive. They just have to get the clot out and change her medications. She's a fighter, this won't take long and she'll be back on the road to recovery."

True to the pastor's word, it was a short eternity before they got word that Nicole was out of surgery and in recovery. Not long after that, they got word she was back in her room in the ICU.

They stopped and talked to the doctor, who told them Nicole was going to be fine.

"She needs to rest, so I'd like you all to go home," the doctor said, "but I know that's not going to happen with this group, so here's what I suggest. Pastor, you go in and say your prayer and then leave. Then two of you, only two, go in for about five minutes and then the rest of you all go home. You can come back tomorrow."

"How will this affect her recovery and her pregnancy?" Bonnie asked as Pastor Mark and Rachel went into Nicole's room.

"She should be back on the road to recovery fairly soon. I was planning on moving her into a regular room tomorrow or the next day, so this will delay that for a few days," he said. "It shouldn't affect her pregnancy, but we'll monitor it closely. I'll consult with her OB/GYN. We were keeping her blood thinners at a minimal dose because of the pregnancy, and she got the clot, so now we'll try to set an optimum dose."

"Thanks, doctor," Bonnie said.

As soon as Pastor Mark and Rachel came out and said their goodbyes, David and Bonnie went in to visit.

"How are you, honey?" Bonnie asked, gently taking Nicole's hand.

"I'm drowsy and the incision hurts a bit, but I'm fine," she murmured. "But I am worried about the baby."

"We all are," David told her, patting her other hand. "But the doctor seems to think it will be okay. You relax and try to get some sleep and we'll see you in the morning."

Chapter Four

"Surely he hath borne our griefs, and carried our sorrows: yet we did esteem him stricken, smitten of God, and afflicted. But he was wounded for our transgressions, he was bruised for our iniquities: the chastisement of our peace was upon him; and with his stripes we are healed."
(Isaiah 53:4-5)

The next few weeks were a blur, filled with constant treatments including plastic surgeries and painful wound care. To top it off, a few days after her surgery for the pulmonary embolism she was moved to a regular room. Once she was in that room her physical therapy began. The physical therapy sessions, conducted under the care of a physical therapist named Troy, were pure torture. She had lost so much muscle tone and mobility it was amazing, but Troy the Terrible, as she thought of him, pushed her to regain her former strength. He was relentless and demanding, but he was also, in a strange way, very gentle with her. For the first few days, he came to her room, massaging and articulating her limbs. He walked beside her, up and down the hallway outside her room. After a few days the sessions with Troy were moved down to a basement floor. There was a gym, but some of the equipment was very strange to Nicole. Troy always put her through a long hard workout, and each day he expected her to show some improvement. The sessions took up most of her mornings and left her feeling weak and exhausted.

For the rest of the day there was boredom, pain, and almost constant nurses, lab techs and doctors. They took her blood so often she wondered if there was any left in her. Her only relief from all of this was her frequent visitors. Now that she was in a regular room it was open season on visitors. Her room became filled with gifts and flowers. Every few days she had most of the flowers sent to other rooms. She knew there were some patients who didn't get very many.

Still, as Nicole continued to heal she began to slip into a major depression. The losses got to her; her murdered friends, her job and career, and her innocence... all gone! She was also having violent nightmares. The doctors offered to give her sleeping pills but she refused, worrying about the effect it might have on her baby. Although she was healing and she had lots of guests, she felt restless and tired. To add insult to, well, injury, she had morning sickness that no medication seemed to help. She began each day with mild tea and crackers.

The visitors were the only bright spots in her day, and Nicole had lots of visitors. Pastor Mark and Rachel, along with many members of the church came often and prayed with her. Pastor Brad from Emily's church visited several times too. They would read passages from the Bible, pray, and just sit and talk. Some of those church ladies could even get Nicole to laugh. They weren't stuffy, those church ladies, they all really had a sense of humor. Rachel, the Pastor's wife, was always ready with her warm, genuine smile and a soft hug. The only problem was finding a place to hug that didn't hurt.

One memorable day Emily brought her mother with her to visit Nicole at the hospital. Julia, the nurse, had a trip she had been planning to go on for a long time and Emily told her to go on and have fun. Emily had been fighting the flu and it was her first visit since Nicole had been moved to a regular room, so Emily had to hunt her down with Mae in tow.

Just getting Mae out of the house and loaded into the car was an adventure. Mae wanted to go to Disneyland and didn't know anyone named Nicole anyway! Emily and Mae finally got to the hospital and they found Nicole's new room. Mae sat in a chair beside Nicole and chatted with her, almost making sense. Nicole chatted right back to her, playing off whatever Mae said.

Mae talked on and on, her pale blue eyes flashing. As she spoke her fine hair fell out of its bun, covering her face in a soft, gray cloud.

"Why did you choose this hotel?" Mae asked, irritated. "The room service here is terrible!"

Nicole nodded wisely. "The room service is indeed terrible and they don't even have a pool!"

Emily just laughed.

On other days her friends Kate and Laura came, sometimes with kids and husbands and sometimes just themselves. When either Kate or Laura brought their kids things got pretty wild. Kate had five children, three from her first husband and two more from her current husband, Bob, all under seven, and she would bring a sitter. Once the kids said hi to Nicole, the sitter bravely took the brood, along with their coloring books, to the cafeteria. Laura's twins were about two, and she only brought them once. Her husband, Jack, wrangled the pair and once again the cafeteria was the best place for them. For the most part, Kate and Laura just came by themselves.

Those visits were a bit of both relief and trauma for Nicole. Kate and Laura were known for one peculiar habit of theirs. They were really into matchmaking, an area in which they were ruthless and strangely infallible. Nicole had often wondered why they had never set her up, but she had never asked. Still, she enjoyed watching them work. Sometimes their husbands came with them and watched as they matched up various members of the hospital staff.

It was during one of the visits that included their husbands where Kate met the young investigator, Detective Reynolds. She noticed how professional he was, how well his tight jeans molded to his body, and she also saw his interest in Nicole. She met Laura's eyes and they watched him for a while. They noted his patience with Nicole, his quiet manners, so unlike the stereotypical cop; and how he seemed eager to cater to her needs.

Suddenly Kate cocked an eyebrow and swung her eyes to meet Laura's.

Kate's husband, Bob, caught the look and pulled the two aside. "Are you two matchmaking again? Don't you ever stop? But hey, even I can tell he's interested in her. This would be a piece of cake."

Kate kissed her husband quickly. "No, love, he's not the one. Not for Nicole."

Bob walked over to ask Laura, "Dare I ask why?"

"Because he's still focusing on Nikki Silver, not Nicole Silvan. He sees her as wounded, and he expects her to heal." Laura paused. "I think his interest is genuine but it's not based on the woman she really is, it's based on the image of the woman she was."

Before long, Nicole's OB/GYN came in to check on her. She was a resident, about 30 years old, with caramel skin, caring brown eyes and a wide smile. The detective's eyes went straight to her. Her name badge read Dr. Wendy Sullivan.

"Doctor Sullivan, how nice to meet you at last. We've been wondering when we would get the chance since you always seem to come check on Nick when we're not around," Laura said.

"That's because I was warned about you two, the matchmakers, as you're known around here. At least three nurses and two doctors said you set them up. Now they're all dating, engaged, or even married. But they are all very happy and in love. But see here, I'm still a resident, I cannot afford to fall in love just yet, not for my career, not emotionally, and not financially." She smiled good-naturedly. "So back off, don't even try."

"We wouldn't dream of it." Laura hid her grin, she loved being challenged. "Dr. Sullivan, have you met Detective Reynolds? He's one of the detectives investigating Nicole's attack."

The doctor shot Laura a resigned sneer, then slid her gaze over to Detective Reynolds. He was blushing! She smiled softly, not bad, not bad at all.

"Witch!" Kate whispered to Laura, mocking her in a singsong voice as they left the room. "I wouldn't dream of setting you up, but please, meet your future husband."

"I'd like to talk to you about Nicole's attack and her condition," the detective said, then took her hand after Kate and Laura left. "If that's all right with Nicole."

He turned to Nicole and saw her nod. "I realize you have to respect doctor/patient confidentiality."

"Well, I need to examine Nicole right now." The doctor smiled, revealing adorable dimples. "How about meeting me in the cafeteria in about 15 minutes?"

"Fine." The detective looked at her even more closely, dimples and deep brown eyes, hmm. "I'll be there."

After he was gone, she sighed and turned to Nicole. "Nicole, I hate to bring up bad memories but I need to verify some things. This pregnancy is a result of rape, correct?"

She looked up to see Nicole nod.

"And murder," Nicole added.

"I personally do not perform abortions, but I have to ask: Are you sure about keeping this baby?" She said it softly.

"Yes, the baby is an innocent." Nicole did not hesitate.

"And have you considered adoption?" She continued, "It might be hard to keep a reminder of the attack."

"I want the child," Nicole said firmly, "however I got it."

She paused, choosing her words. "Please understand, this child shouldn't have been conceived, and shouldn't have survived my injuries and my stress, so this child is here for a reason. He or she is a gift from God to help me move forward from the attack. I truly believe that."

"You're a woman of strong faith then," Doctor Sullivan said. "I am too, so I respect that."

David came bursting into the room. "Hey Nick! I have an idea!'

He leaned in to kiss her cheek, not realizing he was interrupting. "You know Frank's stepdaughter, Cassie?"

Nicole nodded. "She's a little dynamo! How old is she now, anyway?"

"She's ten I think, maybe eleven." David paused. "Anyway, I had a thought, why can't we have her exercise Burgie?"

"Burgie is gentle, but he's also very spirited. Can Cassie handle him?" Nicole frowned both at the thought of someone else riding her horse, and from missing him herself.

David grinned. "I'll work with her, I taught Emily to ride, remember? And she wants to learn gymkhana. She's getting bored with Western Pleasure."

"Correction, I taught Emily to ride, she wanted to surprise you. Still, under your supervision and with her parents' okay, I think it's alright for Cassie to ride Burgie." Nicole rubbed her growing belly gently. "I know my passenger here isn't ready to ride."

Before long, Nicole drifted off to sleep. She'd been dropping off for short naps recently since she started having the nightmares.

Dr. Sullivan looked over as Kate and Laura returned. "Ms. Silvan must be a great lady, all of the nurses say she's very nice, even in her pain. I understand she's a famous model."

"She was. I doubt that she'll be going back to modeling, but yes, she's Nikki Silver," Laura said. "Please call her Nicole, or Nick."

"She wants the baby, really wants it, so I'm going to do my best for her," the doctor assured Nicole's friends.

"We know you will," David told her, "and it will help that Nicole's not a difficult patient. She'll follow doctor's orders."

"Well, I'd better go meet that detective for coffee." The doctor turned and smiled at Kate and Laura. "I know your game, I seem to have been set up by some champion matchmakers. Just don't expect me to go along like a lamb to the slaughter."

"His first name's Sam," Kate called out after the doctor's retreating back.

Laura just laughed and added, "Name the first baby after one of us."

They heard a muffled shriek coming from down the hall. "That's not funny!"

"Hey!" Nicole laughed as she protested from the bed. "Don't go matchmaking with all my admirers, leave at least one for me. My ego's a little bruised right now."

"He wasn't the right one," Laura said dismissively. "Trust me."

Having heard that phrase from Laura hundreds of times, Nick could only sigh and sink back into sleep.

The matchmaking continued. It was almost a legend among the hospital staff, but there was a division among those eager to find true love and those who were trying to avoid being caught.

One of her other doctors, her plastic surgeon, was a brilliant man in his mid-thirties, Dr. Simon Haskell. He also seemed to be interested in Nicole. He was a single man with blond hair and green eyes, and a harried manner. During his frequent visits he tried to maintain a professional bedside manner, but his interest was apparent. His eyes lit up as he spoke to her, often holding her hand without realizing it. His smile seemed glued to her face, his manner was almost too gentle. He always had one more surgery to suggest, one more treatment.

Nicole had seen many men interested in her over the years and was well aware of the signs. Even though she thought her scars had ended that part of her life, she was reassured by the doctor's attention. That is, she was reassured right up to the moment when Laura and Kate, who were visiting along with their friend Lanie, caught sight of him. Lanie was the mother of the girl who was going to start exercising Nicole's horse, and she wanted to get to know her better.

Dr. Haskell stopped in Nicole's room just for a moment,

checking on the results of her last procedure, as well as the progress of her healing. He barely got started when his pager suddenly went off.

"I'm sorry, Nicole, I'm needed in the ER. I'll be back, probably in about an hour." He rushed out.

As soon as he'd left the room, Laura gave Kate the look.

"Lanie," Kate said casually, "why don't you call your sister Tina and have her meet us here?"

"Gee, you two," Nicole said sarcastically, "I find another man who can see past the scars and now you're planning to set him up."

Lanie was already on her cell phone. Having gotten married as a result of a Kate and Laura set-up, she knew what they had in mind. She also knew love didn't always come easily because she'd fought the set-up tooth and nail and almost had to be dragged to the altar kicking and screaming. She was now very happily married.

"I know, I know," Nicole added before Laura could open her mouth, "he's not the one, trust me."

"I think she's onto us," Kate said in a stage whisper, behind her hand.

Laura just laughed.

Nicole went into a minor sulk, two men, two, who were attracted to her in spite of her scars, and Kate and Laura set them both up with other women. Traitors! She glared at them but they seemed oblivious.

Lanie's sister arrived at the hospital, looking fabulous. She had a dress that set off her curvy figure without being obvious. Her blonde hair was piled in a flattering mass on top of her head with a few tendrils trailing down. And since she'd been doing a lot of outdoor work her freckles were, well, covering her face.

Dr. Haskell came back from his call. "I'm back, Nicole. Let me look at you and see how those burn scars are doing before I get called away again." He looked her over, making small hems and haws as he explored her body. "I think we can do more for your face and neck, but from the neck down, I think we should let it be, at least for now."

Nicole's burns mainly ran down the left side of her body. Her face and her neck were the least scarred, and her chest had a shiny, melted wax appearance. From the chest down, the left side of her body was more scarred.

After the doctor finished his exam he stood up and acknowledged the others in the room for the first time. "Hi, I didn't mean to ignore you guys, but I was focusing on my patient. She's doing really well. I want you to know I'm consulting with surgeons all over the world for the latest treatment of burn scars. There will be some residual scarring, of course, but I'll do what I can."

"Thanks, Doctor," Kate said. "We know you'll do your best for her. Have you met our friend, Tina?"

Tina met the doctor's eyes, and he returned the gaze. There was a zing in the room that was almost palpable. "Nice to meet you, Tina."

"Doctor, you should know, we're being set up." Tina was a frank girl. "Kate and Laura are matchmakers."

The doctor turned and winked at Kate and Laura. "Good job! Darn good job."

Nicole groaned as she sank back on the bed. Her second admirer was gone! At this rate she'd be an old maid. She glared at Kate and Laura, who pretended not to notice.

Then the day turned worse as the time for her physical therapy came up. The nurse wheeled her down to a gym in the basement. Nicole groaned as she saw her therapist, Troy Dixon, walk over to her.

The physical therapist had wavy blond hair, a bit longer than most men's but not hitting his shoulders, and he had stern brown eyes. He was a strong man, physically appealing and well-muscled, and firm in his manner. He almost had a drill sergeant mentality as he pushed Nicole extremely hard to regain her strength and mobility. He was careful because of her pregnancy and the severity of her injuries, but still her workouts were very demanding.

"Get out of that chair, you lazy woman." He handed her some dumbbells. "We have work to do."

This was the one admirer she failed to notice. He kept the signs well hidden, but he had fallen head over heels in love with her.

Usually when she went down to PT, Kate and Laura would go to lunch, but one day they decided to follow her down and watch her workout. They saw his no nonsense manner, and how hard he pushed her. They also saw how careful he was of her condition, especially her growing pregnancy. Almost instantly, as they watched the trainer work with her, they turned to each other with grins on their faces.

"This is the one," Kate whispered. "He's perfect!"

"He sure is," Laura agreed. "He's good looking, he knows what's best for Nicole, and he's working hard to give it to her. He pushes her to do her best but he's also very careful because of her pregnancy."

"And it won't be hard to get them together," Kate laughed, as she watched Troy slide a hand gently up Nicole's leg to correct her position.

"Almost too easy." Laura smiled. "No challenge."

Kate and Laura looked at each other and smiled as Laura gave him a thumbs up.

"Hey, Nicole!" Laura whispered in her ear, "We won't chase this one off."

"Troy! Troy?" Shocked, Nicole dropped a weight. "He's inhuman! He's not interested in me, except to torture me."

"Trust me," Kate told her. "Trust me."

"A double trust me? A double? I'm in trouble!" She wiped her forehead with a towel.

Still, she looked at Troy with a fresh eye, not too shabby! And he seemed nice, a drill sergeant, and taciturn, but nice. She shrugged to herself, he had already agreed to work with her in her own gym once she was home.

Chapter Five

"Blessed are they that mourn: for they shall be comforted."
(Matthew 5:4)

A few days later, Lanie brought her daughter, Cassie, to the hospital for a visit. She also brought Nicole a picture of Cassie riding Burgie.

With the innocence of a child, Cassie plopped herself down on the side of the bed. "Wow! You got hurt really bad!" She looked at Nicole with a grin. "Does it still hurt?"

"Not so much now, but they keep doing surgeries to try to hide the scars, and that hurts sometimes." She grinned back at the girl with her slight dusting of freckles and long, fiery red ponytail.

"Mom said I wasn't supposed to mention your scars." Sitting on a chair in the corner, Lanie groaned as Cassie continued. "But you don't look so bad to me."

"Cassie!" Lanie snapped, even though she was trying not to laugh. "Nice job of not mentioning the scars! Sorry, Nicole."

"No problem, Lanie." She turned to Cassie with a puzzled look and a wink. "So what do you think, should I go as Frankenstein for Halloween?"

"More like his bride." Cassie giggled. "Since you're a girl and Frankenstein was a dude."

"Well... that would be closer." Nicole seemed to consider. "But Halloween's a long time away."

"So what are you going to do now?" Cassie asked.

Nicole laughed. "Well, for one thing, I'm not going to model clothes anymore. They don't like scars on fashion models."

"Their loss," Cassie stated firmly. "They always seem to want perfect people to model, and no one's perfect."

Cassie's observation astonished Nicole, coming from a preteen child.

"You're very bright, aren't you?" She stared at Cassie.

"Frank, my new dad, said he can't keep up with me." She looked like an imp. "But he only married Mom about six months ago. I expect he'll learn how I think sooner or later."

Lanie, who was letting Cassie lead the discussion, just laughed. "He still can't figure out how to handle me."

"Oh, I bet he can." Nicole grinned. "That's why you look so happy."

"But other than Halloween, since you can't model anymore," Cassie drew the conversation back to her original question, "what are you going to do? For a job, I mean."

"I have a gym that I'm going to open, to help people gain confidence and feel healthier about themselves. But not just to lose weight." Nicole pushed a button and raised her bed a bit. "What do you think of that?"

"Sounds good to me. Will you allow kids?" Cassie asked.

"I hadn't thought about it because most gyms won't but maybe we can set up some programs and times for kids." Nicole instantly had a few ideas. "Would you like to help me plan some things?"

"Sure, but that's not what I wanted to talk to you about." Uncharacteristically Cassie hesitated.

"What's up kiddo?" Nicole prompted, then took a sip of soda.

"I wanted to thank you for letting me ride Burgie, he's so cool." Cassie was excited. "I love Buddy, my horse, but he's only trained for Western Pleasure Classes, and they're so slow and always the same. Practicing Barrel Racing on Burgie is exciting. He's so fast and his turns are so neat."

"Thank you for riding him while I can't," Nicole said quietly.

"Can I show him sometime? David said it would be up to you." Cassie practically bounced up and down with eagerness. "Mom said not to ask you, but if I don't ask, how will you know I want to?"

There was a choking sound from the corner where Lanie sat. "Cassie."

"Aw, Mom." She was unrepentant. "I had to ask."

"I'll think about it after I'm home," Nicole told her. "After I see how you do on him, fair enough?"

She held out her hand, Cassie took it and grinned. "Okay. Deal!"

Later that day, Detective Reynolds stopped in to update her on the investigation. "We're going through all the emails and letters you received from fans and focusing on the ones that seemed obsessive. Have you remembered anything more?"

"Just what I told you, and that I heard two thumps before something crashed into my head and the lights went out," she answered.

"Autopsy results on the victims showed traces of a knock out drug in their systems, the thumps were probably them falling down," he informed her. "They were probably unconscious..."

"All four of them?" she asked.

"Four? There were only three bodies." The detective hid his excitement, this was new information. "Why did you think four?"

"Well, my hairdresser, make-up, stylist, and the photographer's assistant, Adam." Nicole was puzzled.

"We should have discovered this long ago." Detective Reynolds got out his cell phone and dialed Detective Mollney. "I don't know how we missed it."

When she answered he was excited and urgent. "There were four people there with Nicole, the three vics and a photographer's assistant. Norma, she's seen the suspect!"

After a short conversation the detective turned to Nicole. "Would you be willing to work with a sketch artist?"

"Of course. I want this... this person caught." She was bitter.

"One last thing." He stood up. "Why weren't you drugged like the others?"

"I brought my own coffee in a large mug, along with some bottled water," she explained. "It's just a habit of mine."

"Good habit, as it turns out. I'll send you a sketch artist." He paused. "Also, since we know you can identify the suspect we'll increase your protection."

"I'm practically tripping over the patrolmen guarding me now!" She laughed.

"One thing, do me a favor and please keep Kate and Laura away from my officers." He tried to sound stern. "Three of them are in love, and practically useless."

"And how is Doctor Sullivan?" Nicole laughed at his slight blush.

"Okay, I get it, but this is getting ridiculous." He shrugged. "All these policemen with little red hearts and butterflies floating around their heads. It's embarrassing."

"Just send married officers." She laughed again and shrugged. "Problem solved."

It was after dinner before the sketch artist arrived. She sat with Nicole working on the sketch for about an hour before she came up with a drawing Nicole found acceptable.

"Wow! He's pretty good looking for a murdering rapist!" She studied the final picture. "What a waste. Don't worry, Nicole, we'll catch him soon and then he'll spend the rest of his miserable life in jail. I guarantee you his good looks won't help him there."

The next day her publicist, Shannon Wells, came to the hospital to visit. She had not been in before. It turned out she was not staying away because of a lack of concern, she had simply been very busy in New York and London with major shows.

For a publicist in the fashion industry Shannon sure didn't dress the part unless she was working. Her favored attire was cut off shorts, an oversized T-shirt and sandals, with her long brown hair pulled back in a tail.

"You know how it gets during fashion week, Nicole." She sighed and relaxed. "Crazy, busy, and always filled with last minute problems. I missed you and wanted to be here. You know you were a big topic of conversation around the catwalks. People love you, not just fans, but other models and stylists."

"That's good to know," Nicole admitted. "I was wondering how this was playing out with people who know me, and who knew Hans, Lacey and Ivan. It's weird, but I feel guilty about their murders. I know it wasn't my fault, but I still feel guilty."

"Well," Shannon stood and paced, figuring out how to convince Nicole to go along with her idea, "I have an idea I think you're going to hate, but please hear me out."

She explained how she was handling reports in the media about Nicole's injuries.

"I really think you need to do an interview." She was convincing. "A radio interview if you'd prefer. We could even do it here, in this hospital room. And of course if you're still shy about showing your scars, radio is the best way to go."

"If I did it, this interview would have to be more about my friends, who were innocent victims of the attack, than about my looks. My looks are unimportant and insignificant compared to their lives. This attack was painful, degrading, and its effects are still coming to light."

"What do you mean?" Shannon asked. "What is still coming to light?"

Nicole paused, knowing Shannon did not share her beliefs on abortion, although she'd tried to convince her. "Well, Shannon, for one thing, I'm pregnant, by my rapist."

"What!" Shannon was stunned. "Even you must admit it, you can't have this monster's baby."

"I am. I'm having my baby, and raising it with love." Nicole smiled at her shocked friend. "What has this baby done to deserve the death penalty? I'm looking at this baby as a gift from God, to help erase the terror and horror of the attack."

"It's your choice," Shannon admitted, "and it's a brave choice. I will admit I do admire your courage and your faith. Now about the interview, how would you feel about doing it with Shelby Newsome? She's interviewed you before."

"I remember the interview with Shelby. I liked her as a person." Nicole remembered. "Since I did like her and feel comfortable with her, I'll agree to Shelby."

Later that day Nicole got a call from the police. The suspect had been identified, his name was Adam Hannan. He was a radical Muslim and had a history of violence against women. The reason he had slipped under the radar screen was because his attacks were spread out over several states, even other countries, and the cases had never been connected before. Most of his friends and family thought he was a quiet, decent man and refused to help the police find him. To make it worse, he'd gone into hiding. Some reports had him in Canada, some in New York, others in Michigan, and some even put him in the Middle East.

The next few days went by slowly, waiting for word about the suspect and hoping for his arrest. She had her morning sessions with Troy, who teased and nagged her into putting out greater and greater effort in her workouts. He was always ready to rub her neck or massage her sore calves. He always had a warm smile for her just before he tortured her.

Finally the day for the interview arrived. First a sound technician came into the room to make sure everything was ready for the interview. Then Shelby came bustling in, cordless microphone in one hand, and an earpiece in one ear.

Once she arrived, Shelby was shocked to see Nicole. In spite of knowing what had happened to her, the scars caught her off guard.

"Oh my God, you poor thing!" she gushed, tears forming in her hazel eyes. "How could such a terrible..."

She stopped and caught herself. "I'm sorry that was unprofessional."

"No problem. I've always wondered how reporters can see the things they see every day and not be moved," Nicole assured her with a grin. "Now I know you're human."

"Oh, I'm human alright," Shelby said slowly. "And you are a walking, talking illustration of one of my secret fears."

"What do you mean?" Nicole puzzled.

"I've had a stalker and a few crazed fans. It's a fact of life when you're in the public eye," Shelby admitted. "I'm not as famous as you but I am on air, on the evening news, and I get some crazies. So I can relate a little."

"Thank God you haven't been injured," Nicole whispered. "It seems unreal, except the loss of my friends and the pain."

Well, before we talk it to death between ourselves, let's put this on air. We're taping this now to be aired at 8 PM." Shelby took a deep breath and turned on her microphone. "Let's get started."

She nodded to Nicole. "Hi, this is Shelby Newsome. I'm here with Nikki Silver who's still in the hospital recovering from a terrible attack, that left five people dead."

She paused. "Hi, Nikki, how are you feeling after your tragic attack?"

"I'm getting better, I've lost some strength and coordination, so it's slow, but I am healing. What happened to me was bad enough, Shelby, but I lived," Nicole replied, sadly. "More important than what happened to me, three of my friends and a photographer's assistant did not."

At the insistence of the detectives, Nicole kept quiet about the suspect. She would have anyway. She knew enough not to let it get out that she knew who the attacker was, even though the police were hunting him.

"And my manager was murdered on the same day, but in a separate location," she continued. "That's far more important, far worse than what happened to me; all I lost was my career, several very good people, friends of mine, lost their lives."

"Nicole, please tell the people how your career was lost," Shelby interrupted.

"I've been burned, and it left me badly scarred," Nicole told the listeners. "I don't know of any model who's worked with this much scarring. But as I was saying, what happened to me is not important. What happened to my friends and co-workers was devastating. They did nothing, nothing to deserve what happened to them. Their families did nothing wrong. They were all decent people, all devout Christians, at least the ones I knew. I'd never met the assistant before."

"Do you know what was behind the attack?" Shelby asked.

"The police think it was probably an obsessed fan," Nicole told her. "It's pretty plain I was the target."

"How is that plain?" the reporter asked.

For an answer, Nicole stood, showing her small pregnancy belly. "I was the one he raped."

"So that baby is the attacker's child?" Shelby asked.

"Yes, I've been a Christian for years, and although not everyone does it nowadays, I was saving myself for marriage. I was a virgin before this." Nicole sat back down. "As hard as that will be for some people to believe. They think a model lives a wild life, filled with travel, luxury, and parties. We don't. Most of us work too hard for that. Now I'm pregnant and I don't even remember what happened."

"And you're keeping the baby? No abortion, no adoption?" Shelby let her shock show in her voice.

Nicole held her head high, and raised her voice slightly.

"This is my child. Should I kill it? And adoption can be a great choice, but this," she rubbed her belly, "this is mine, and I will love him or her. I choose to believe this baby is a gift from God, so that something wonderful can come out of something horrible."

"What about the baby's father? What do you think should happen to him?" Shelby demanded.

"He should be arrested, tried, and sentenced to the rest of his life in prison, without parole." She was firm.

"No forgiveness then?" the reporter asked. "I thought Christians were supposed to forgive."

"We do. But you're also wrong. I'm working on forgiving him and I will succeed. It isn't easy, but I will forgive him. I already pray for him," Nicole said firmly. "That does not negate the punishment for five murders, one attempted murder, and rape."

"You seem remarkably strong and level-headed for someone who's gone through so much, how do you account for that?" Shelby asked.

"I've had my bad days, my anger, my depression, the sense of loss, plenty of bad days and more pain than I can describe," Nicole admitted. "Part of whatever strength I have, a small part, is my professional experience at hiding any problems or pain behind my smile. A larger part of it is the prayers and support from my friends, my family, and my church. Most of it comes from my faith in Jesus."

"Didn't Jesus let you down," Shelby asked, "by allowing this to happen to you?"

"No, bad things can happen to anyone, on any day. After all, Satan is alive and active. There are also people who use free will to make bad choices. Of course, anyone can become ill or be in an accident. Even with God, those things can happen."

"Then what does your faith in Jesus do for you?" Shelby asked, genuinely curious.

"He gives me the strength to go on, to do more than recover. I will triumph, watch and see. My child will be a blessing to me," Nicole said with conviction. "Christ will find ways to use me for His glory, to inspire others who may be hurt or suffering. Something fantastic will come of this, I know it."

"Right now, what's your biggest frustration?" Shelby decided to wrap up the interview.

Nicole's smile lit up her face. "That's easy, I want to go

home!"

Shelby wrapped up her part of the interview by saying, "We can never forget those who were murdered for one man's obsession, but you've already turned a tragedy, at least your part of that tragedy, into a triumph of the human spirit. Your strength is an inspiration to anyone who gets knocked out by life. You say your friends and your faith have given you strength. Your friends must be terrific. Your faith is strong and deep. Many people find strength in adversity, but to me you are astonishing, and that is a testament to your belief in God. You humble me."

Shelby was overcome with emotion as she gave Nicole a hug, then left.

For several weeks after her radio interview and the transcript was posted online, Nicole received reactions from her fans and the public in general. She got piles of letters and cards, even gifts and flowers. Most were favorable, some even called her a saint. That bothered Nicole, who saw herself as just being someone who was trying to do the right thing.

The ones that really bothered her, however, were the ones who called her vile names and said she deserved what he did to her. She couldn't understand them, but they hurt.

Chapter Six

"And he sent them to preach the kingdom of God, and to heal the sick."
(Luke 9:2)

Surprisingly, one of Nicole's most fervent prayers was answered the next day. Dr. Sullivan told her she could go home. She was so excited, it felt like she was being paroled from prison, a prison where she was constantly poked and prodded, stuck with needles and cared for, but a prison nevertheless. She was ecstatic as she called David.

David was working in his office with a meeting scheduled for later in the day. He called his client, who knew Nicole, and told her he had to reschedule. The client agreed, and asked him to give Nicole her best wishes. He called Emily to make sure her room was ready. Then he took the rest of the day off from work and came to get her.

Nicole had gifts and flowers scattered all over the room. She told the nurses to give the flowers that still looked good to patients who didn't have very many. She'd already given out most of them anyway.

Some of the gifts were things like teddy bears, and she had those sent to the pediatric ward. David packed up her nighties and robe, slippers, her grooming items, and whatever else he could find that belonged to Nicole. He walked beside her as a nurse rolled her out to his car in a wheelchair.

When Nicole got home from the hospital, Mae met her at the door. She took one look at Nicole's scars and started to weep, her arms going gently around Nicole's waist.

"Oh, baby," she said as she wept, "who hurt you? I'll kill 'em!"

The idea of a 75-year-old, 90 pound, fragile Mae actually hurting anyone almost made Nicole laugh.

A few days later, Mae's reaction was entirely different.

She looked at Nicole and said sternly, "You young people today, I just do not get this make-up. It's not pretty. It looks like a Halloween costume."

"Mae, it's not make-up, it's real scars," Nicole told her gently. "I was injured in an accident."

"Well, of course you were," Mae said indignantly, and then followed it a few moments later with, "Who are you?"

"I'm Nicole, David's sister." Nicole squeezed her eyes shut.

"Oh, I remember." Julia came into the room and hustled Mae off to their suite.

"Emily, I love your mom, but she wears me out." Nicole turned to Emily with a rueful smile.

"Me too," Emily admitted. "Why don't you sit on the porch and I'll bring you something to drink. Iced tea? Lemonade?"

"Thanks Em." Nicole smiled. "I'll take lemonade."

In a few minutes, both women were sitting outside in the cool evening breeze, sipping lemonade and relaxing. To Nicole, it felt like pure heaven. She hadn't been outside in months.

Now that she was home, Nicole gradually grew stronger, and as she did, her spirit came back. A big part of her recovery was just being home. Because they had an RN living in the house, she was discharged a little earlier than she would have been without Julia.

A few weeks after Nicole's return from the hospital, she noticed Mae watching her from around corners. Mae would cock her neck and study Nicole. Finally Nicole had enough.

"Mae, why are you staring at me?" Nicole asked her outright, but with a gentle tone.

"I was just wondering," Mae replied. "Can't blame me for wondering, can you?"

"Wondering what?" Nicole puzzled. "I'll tell you if I can."

"Just how many babies do you have in there anyway?" Mae demanded.

"When the doctor tells me, I'll tell you, okay?" Nicole laughed.

A few days after Nicole got home, Troy began coming to the house to work with her in the evenings after he finished his shift at the hospital. He put her through all of her physical therapy in her own gym, sometimes followed by a swim in the pool. He was never easy on her, still he was careful, but never easy. He pushed her to work as hard as she could in spite of her growing pregnancy.

"You want to be strong to take care of that baby, don't you?" He handed her a five pound weight.

"Of course I do." Nicole began doing arm curls with the weight. "But I wonder..."

"Wonder what?" Troy was puzzled.

"Why don't all women need a sadistic drill sergeant to get ready to care for newborn babies?" She put down the weight and sipped her water before wiping her face with a towel.

"Hey!" Troy reacted. "I'm not that bad! Am I?"

"Yes." Nicole relented and said, "But I do appreciate it."

"Everything I do with you now will only make your pregnancy and labor easier," he pointed out.

"I'm all for easier labor and a safe delivery." Nicole moved to the treadmill. "This baby is all I have now. Well, along with my family and my horse."

Troy never let his feelings for her show; although as he was working with her he often used his hands to correct her position and help her with the exercises. At the end of her daily therapy, Troy often rubbed out her aches and pains. She, somehow, seemed to have a lot of aches and pains.

After her workout the two of them would go for a short swim, then she would let the horses out to run around the arena. He would sit with her and watch the horses run around and then roll in the dirt. It always amused him watching each horse walk around, pawing and sniffing the ground. It was as if choosing exactly where to roll was the most important decision of their equine day. Maybe it was, he thought.

Several days a week, Nicole sat out by the arena and watched Cassie ride her horse, Burgie. Troy noticed it was rough on her because she wanted to ride. Nicole pleaded with Troy and asked him if he would take her riding. She really missed being on her horse but he refused until she had it cleared with her doctor. She promised him she would check with the doctor during her next visit.

Still, Burgie needed a good, hard workout. Cassie was getting good at basic gymkhana events, barrel racing, single pole and pole bending. She still ran the events at about half speed, but her turns were smooth. Nicole knew it was time for the girl to pick up the pace.

One day as she waited while Cassie saddled Burgie, she called the girl over. "Cassie, come here a minute. Let David check the girth."

David did, and saddled his horse as well.

Cassie bounded over. "Hey Nicole, what's up?"

"I just wanted to thank you again for riding Burgie for me. I can't ride yet, and we don't want him getting lazy, do we?" Nicole blocked the sun with one hand.

"I'm having fun!" Cassie grinned, and then looked at Nicole. "Do you want to hear something strange?"

"Sure, what?"

"I hope you don't get mad at me for saying this but when I saw you at the hospital, at first, all I could see was your scars," she said softly. "Now I look at you and just see Nicole."

Nicole was choked up for a minute before she said, "Thank you, I needed to hear that. Now here's something you need to hear: I want you to go faster on the barrels, single poles, and poles today. Let him run. Push him. You're ready."

Cassie climbed on Burgie and began to warm him up, walking him for a while before moving him into a jog, then an extended trot, and finally a canter. She worked a few rollbacks along the rail. At Nicole's nod, she lined Burgie up for single pole and ran the event. She did well. She was still not going full speed, but much faster.

David did likewise with Target. Cassie worked single pole twice more, increasing her speed each time. David ran it one more time, then dismounted and handed his reins to Cassie and set up barrels.

They both ran barrels and once again Cassie's time was faster than ever. This time she only ran it once before David set up pole bending. Cassie was doing really well. After that, he set up a new event for Cassie, quadrangle. She did well on everything, but was slower with Quad. Cassie unsaddled both horses, washing off the sweat and putting them on the hot walker. David went up to the house and brought her a cold soda. She sat under the trees and waited for her mom to come get her.

Not long after her return home, Nicole had an appointment with Dr. Sullivan. The doctor checked Nicole over completely and then they sat down for a chat. The doctor soon learned that Nicole was becoming restless. She felt tied down, surrounded by friends, family and the police, but still afraid to leave her house. Her fear wasn't all for herself, since her friends had been murdered she was afraid for her family and the people who surrounded her. That was why she hadn't returned to church yet.

She did have a request for the doctor, she wanted permission to ride her horse. She was ready to beg and plead for the doctor's permission.

"I know that I can only ride at a walk," she told the doctor. "But even walking would give me a sense of freedom. I can walk around in the arena or go out on the trail, with some protection. I can't wait to ride Burgie."

She knew that even riding at a walk would feel wonderful, and free. It would also give her a sense that she was really beginning to heal, mentally as well as physically.

"I promise, Doctor, I'll be very careful." She meant every word. "If I have even a hint of anything wrong I won't ride."

"Most doctors today feel that moderate exercise is good for a pregnant woman," the doctor said, considering. "Especially if the exercise is something you're used to doing, but in your case, you've been through a lot with your injuries and you haven't ridden in a long time... Still, I think if you're extremely careful and let someone else saddle the horse, you should be okay."

Nicole was shocked and surprised that Dr. Sullivan had given her permission.

Troy began to ride with Nicole, usually in the arena, but sometimes with a police escort, they would go out on a short trail ride. Being on Burgie was a thrill, especially when they went out on the trail. It made her feel like she was really getting well. Troy rode beside her on Emily's horse, Raider, and having him there was wonderful. He made her feel protected and cared for. She was glad some of the police officers guarding her knew how to ride. Some days, instead of working in the gym she and Troy would just ride the horses for a while, then go for a swim followed by a picnic on the lawn.

Troy usually stayed for dinner after he worked with Nicole. He really fit in well with the family, and they all grew to like him. Since the weather was so warm, Troy and Nicole often took a swim in the pool and laid out on the warm grass. They chatted and laughed but kept things on an easy level, light and casual. Neither of them really knew how much the other enjoyed those visits. Nicole still felt the weight of the scars and lacked confidence. Troy was just a quiet man.

As her pregnancy developed, Nicole began to look forward to the birth of her baby. As the baby began to move within her, she was startled to feel her love for the baby grow.

Another day, Nicole called Cassie over as she finished riding.

"Hey, Cassie, good job! Come over here I have something you might like."

As Cassie came close enough, Nicole took her hand and placed it on her swollen belly.

Cassie's eyes grew rounder. "Wow! What's he doing in there?"

"Troy says it's kickboxing, but I think it's soccer." Nicole laughed.

On her next visit to the doctor, Dr. Sullivan did more tests on Nicole. She was a little surprised and concerned at how big Nicole was getting. As they talked after the exam, she told Nicole that on her next visit, they would do an ultrasound.

"The baby has started kicking," Nicole told her doctor. "He or she is a future soccer player."

Still, with all the doctor visits and physical therapy sessions, Nicole was restless. She had visitors almost daily but because of the danger, she stayed home. She felt trapped. Her memories of the attack began to return, and that was the worst thing of all. She woke up in a cold sweat some nights, or with a nightmare that was all too real.

The two detectives came over to the ranch several times to talk about the case and see how Nicole was doing. They told her they had several clues they were following. They also reassured her about the protection they had surrounding her since the attacker was still on the loose.

They didn't tell her everything, however. They didn't tell her about the clues they found from the letters David had in his files from her obsessed fans. They also didn't tell her about the witnesses who saw Adam leaving right before the fire blazed out of control. They didn't tell her that the bodies that were found had traces of an accelerator on their bodies. Adam, when he set the fire, fully intended for them all to die.

When the day came for the ultrasound Nicole was very excited. She couldn't wait to find out if her baby was healthy and what sex it was. She got a very big surprise when the doctor and technician told her she had twins.

"Do you want to know what sex they are?" Dr. Sullivan asked.

"Yes, I do." Nicole grinned and gently rubbed her belly. "Although I don't know what difference it would make, I'll love them anyway."

"Well it's early, but it looks like you're having a boy and a girl," the doctor said. "Does that make you happy?"

"It sure does." Nicole wept a few gentle tears of joy before she dressed, picked up her purse and got ready to leave. "Thanks, Doc."

One day Shelby gave Nicole a call and asked if she could come visit. That afternoon she came out to the ranch and got out of her car. Nicole was sitting on the porch at the big picnic table and had lemonade and some fresh homemade cookies waiting. She and Shelby sat and talked.

"Boy! You've really healed." Shelby was enthusiastic. "You look so much better."

"I have come a long way. I feel very much better. I'll still have some scars, but I do feel well." Nicole reached for the lemonade. "And my pregnancy, well, as you can see, I'm getting bigger."

"You seem happy." Shelby took a cookie.

"I am." Nicole stretched out her legs on the bench. "I have to be careful because he's still out there. Also, I still have some operations to go through, and I still need physical therapy, but I was the lucky one, some good people are dead. You know, some people think coming out of a coma is like, um, Sleeping Beauty waking up, still beautiful and in the same shape she was in when she went to sleep. It's not like that, you wake up weak, and have to build your strength back, and learn how to do things like writing or walking all over again."

She stopped talking and looked directly at Shelby. "Shelby? I'm glad to see you, but what did you have in mind when you came here today?"

"Well, I did want to see how you were getting on." Shelby smiled and bit into a cookie. "These are really good. I also did have a second reason for coming today. I was approached by some people who are starting a campaign about ending violence against women and they were looking for a spokesperson. I instantly thought of you. Who could be more perfect?"

"I'll have to think about that. I want to do the right thing, but what is the right thing? What's right for my babies? And what's the right thing for other women? And I want to think about how I'd feel putting my face out in front of the public again. I want to know if this organization is Christian, and if it is pro-life." Nicole stood and started pacing the small porch, thinking even as she was speaking.

"It just seemed to me," Shelby said, "that this was a great way for you to turn your tragedy into a triumph and help other people at the same time. And hey, did you say babies?"

"I sure did, I'm having twins, a boy and a girl. Now about this campaign, it sure does sound like a great way to use my situation. I'll probably do it," Nicole admitted, "but I want to research this organization, that's something I've learned from this incident. I also want to discuss this with the police and my family, and pray over the idea with my pastor."

Shelby stood up and reached into her purse to give Nicole a card. "Think it over and call these people." Shelby left.

The next day the detectives stopped in, she discussed the idea with them. They thought it was a good idea for her to appear as a spokesperson against violence and told her they would make sure she was safe whenever she did any public service announcements or promotional spots.

Pastor Mark came by several times to counsel and pray with Nicole, so it was easy for her to discuss the plan for the campaign against violence with him. She felt like it was a good idea and a way for her to turn her tragedy into a victory, but she wanted his input. They discussed the idea, including her feelings about exposing her scars and pregnancy to the public. They also discussed the need for security since her attacker was still loose and unknown. Pastor Mark reminded her that her safety was important for herself and for the baby. He was delighted when she corrected him and made baby into babies. As they prayed together, Nicole came to her decision. She would do the campaign.

The one who seemed not to care if it was one baby or twins was Troy. He just pushed her through her workouts even harder.

As her recovery moved on, Nicole was getting tired of being with Troy and not saying anything about her feelings for him, even worse, she was getting tired of Troy not saying anything about his feelings for her. Nicole was not a woman used to being quiet about her feelings for very long. That hadn't changed since the fire. She decided to take matters into her own hands. They were sitting by the arena, watching the horses run loose when she decided to act.

"Troy," Nicole looked into his eyes, "I have a few questions for you."

"What is it, Nicole?" Troy looked at her seriously.

"First of all, how do you feel about me? Do you care for me as a person, as a friend, or as a woman?" Nicole demanded. "Am I just a patient to you or do you have real feelings for me?"

"Nicole, I've tried to be professional but it's hard because I do care for you, in fact I'm in love with you." Troy shifted his feet uncomfortably with his head down, then looked up and met Nicole's eyes. "So I have to ask you, the same question. How do you feel about me?"

"Before I can answer that Troy, I need to ask you one more thing: how do you feel about my babies?" She met his eyes directly. "I need to know that you could love my children in spite of how I came to have them."

"If I'm with you, I would love your babies as if they were my own," Troy said softly. "I'd be proud to act as a father for them."

"Then I must admit I love you too." Nicole smiled softly. "Thank God, so kiss me you fool."

And he did. He really did. Wow!

"I must admit," Nicole said as she snuggled in his arms, "I was afraid no man would ever find me attractive again until you came into my life."

"Nicole," he hugged her just a little bit tighter, "you are beautiful in my eyes. I'm sure that you are beautiful in the Lord's eyes, too."

Nicole savored the moment and Troy's words, then she had another question. "Troy, can you help me get trained as a physical therapist? I want to change the focus of my new gym and add physical therapy to the mix. I've already added some children's classes like swimming, dance exercise, and karate."

"Of course, sweetie." Troy wrapped his arms around her in a warm hug, a big grin spreading all over his face. He kissed her again.

"And one more question." Nicole looked up at him shyly. "Troy will you-" She stopped talking as Troy put one finger over her lips.

"Let me be the one to ask this question," Troy said firmly. "Nicole, would you please marry me?"

"Yes!"

Chapter Seven

"Behold I send you forth, as sheep in the midst of wolves: be ye therefore wise as serpents, and harmless as doves."
(Matthew 10:16)

After talking to her pastor and family, Nicole called Shelby and set up an informal meeting with her. She had decided to do the public service campaign. Since she had become friends with Shelby, she told her to bring her swimsuit so that they could relax and take a swim together. After a quick swim and some iced tea on the porch, she let Shelby know that she had thought it over and talked it over with her pastor, even prayed about it with him, and decided to do the campaign.

Now she wanted Shelby to set up a meeting for her with the group behind the campaign, Speak Out to End Domestic Violence, to be certain that their vision of the campaign matched hers. She wanted to be sure they knew she was pregnant and keeping her babies, and that they knew she was a strong Christian who would bring her faith in God and Christ into her messages for the campaign. To her relief, they felt the same way she did.

They decided that she would do a series of public service announcements and a full half hour on air interview. For the interview, Nicole requested, and the group agreed, that they use Shelby as the interviewer. They also decided that Nicole would not use a prepared script, but would answer questions from Shelby and then speak about her experiences from the heart.

On the day of the interview, Nicole spent quite a bit of time getting herself ready. She was nervous about her first public appearance since being burned. She wore a summer print dress, one that covered her fairly well. She brushed out her long, blonde hair leaving it straight and flowing, although it was noticeably shorter on one side. She used light make-up to highlight her eyes and set off her cheeks and lips. She looked at the finished product in her mirror. She looked as good as she could. She sighed, wishing she could cover some of the scars but she also knew their presence would help highlight her story. She was ready, but uncharacteristically nervous. Although it had been less than a year since she was injured, to her it seemed like a lifetime ago. She was experienced as a spokesperson, she'd done countless commercials and endless endorsements but this was different, this was real life.

Troy took her into his arms. "Honey, you look fantastic. You're going to do a lot of good today."

"I hope so." She snuggled into his embrace. "Can we say a prayer before we go?"

"We're running late, let's pray in the car." Troy kissed her quickly.

They walked out to get into her Altima. Troy opened the car door for her.

She drove to the television studio with Troy, and they did indeed say a prayer in the car. One of the policemen went along with them to guard her. It wasn't a long drive to the local TV studio, but Nicole's nerves made it seem much longer, and somehow far too short. She didn't need hair and make-up when she got to the studio, she had done enough herself. She had not even tried to cover her scars since part of her reason for being there was to show what can happen when someone is stalked or victimized by domestic violence. She would face the camera without concealing the scar that ran down one side of her face and neck. Her neckline wasn't low, but it was low enough to show the shiny, puckered skin starting at her collarbone and trailing down to disappear under her neckline.

On the screen behind Shelby, they had a picture of Nicole from her modeling days, it was a spectacular head shot. Nicole seemed to be making love to the camera; her eyes were full of life, her smile warm and genuine. The light captured her features beautifully. Shelby sat at a desk looking perfectly groomed and beautiful. There was a small, well-screened audience in the studio. Shelby began by talking about what had happened to Nicole.

When the opening was done, Shelby introduced her. "Now, ladies and gentlemen, I'd like to bring out Nikki Silver to tell us about her experiences as a survivor of a violent attack."

As Nicole walked out, the few people allowed into the studio applauded. She sat at the desk opposite Shelby.

"Hi, Shelby," she said calmly. "But I want to correct one thing, I'm not Nikki Silver any longer, I'm Nicole Silvan, now. My modeling career is obviously gone."

"Is that important to you?" Shelby asked.

"No, not at all." Nicole smiled. "I was getting ready to leave the business anyway. What's important to me are the four friends and the photographer's assistant who were murdered by my attacker. I survived, they did not. They are the real tragedy, their families are the most important victims."

"Yes, I can tell you really mean that. Please, tell me in your own words," Shelby said, "what happened to you and how it affected your life."

"Well, I had a fan that was obsessed with me. He wanted to possess me, but he also hated me. He thought all women were worthless, only on earth to bring pleasure to a man. He judged me by my job and decided I was a slut." Nicole's anger and pain came out with every word. "He believes I was without honor and should be put to death."

"I know you, Nicole, and I know just how wrong that fool was," Shelby said quietly but with fervor.

"In fact, I'm a Christian," Nicole started again to tell her tale, she smiled sadly. "Not quite the image of a jet setting fashion model with all those glitzy parties filled with men and liquor, and more. That's how some people see the life of a model. Some girls fit that image, but most do not. Most models work very hard and make it look easy. This... person did not know that. He judged me and found me guilty of having no honor. He set a trap for me and didn't care if he caught some innocent people in that trap."

"How did he set the trap?" Shelby prompted.

"He arranged a phony modeling assignment for me. He even hired three of my friends for my hair, my make-up and as a stylist. At that assignment he murdered those three friends and his assistant, then he raped and tried to murder me. I don't remember all that happened, and even if I did, I wouldn't go into all the details. The fact is three good, decent friends of mine died in the room that day. They were all good Christian people. People who would never hurt anybody, in fact, they all would go out of their way to help someone. But they were slaughtered so that some man could attack me. I didn't know the assistant but he was used to bait the trap and killed too, as was my manager, her throat was slashed in her own home. All that pain and loss for my honor of all things." Nicole gave a grim laugh, devoid of humor. "I know this may be hard for some people to believe, but before the attack I was a virgin."

"A virgin?" Shelby questioned. "Why? At your age."

"I've been a Christian for a long time, and while some people don't believe in celibacy or some give in to temptation, and some just come to accept the Lord after being sexually active, I chose not to be sexually active until marriage. I made that choice for myself, not to judge others."

Nicole smiled softly, but without humor. "And you can tell I'm certainly not a virgin anymore. I am carrying twins, fathered by my rapist, and because I believe abortion is murder I will keep my twins. I will raise them in love and Christianity. I've survived and I will prosper."

She paused for a sip of water. "As hard as it is to believe, I'm engaged now to a good man who doesn't see my scars, doesn't see me as damaged goods, he just loves me. That's a miracle. I love him, and I know he will love my twins, and be a real father to them."

"How did you survive the attack?" Shelby asked.

"I'm told I survived because the only working fire sprinkler in that old building was in the room he dragged me into when he raped me. I think it was a miracle and I was meant to survive." She was firm in her opinion. "After the attack, recovering was the real survival. I used my faith in God to get through the pain, the anger and the depression. It wasn't easy, but I've made it."

Nicole paused. "Once I knew I was going to make it, to survive, I wanted to try to find a way to help people so that no other woman or anyone else would have to go through what I went through. That's why it was a godsend when this opportunity came along. It's perfect for me. I want to try to make sure that no other families ever have to lose somebody over a crazy obsession. I want to warn people to keep their eyes open and follow their feelings."

At a prearranged point, Shelby threw her the question that would let her start the public service announcement. To answer it, Nicole went into the part of the interview that would be used in her 30 second public service announcement.

"So what advice do you have for anyone who might be in danger?"

"Please be careful and aware, if somebody shows signs of violence or obsession towards you get away from them. Value yourself and your friends far too much to fall into the trap of being a victim to violence. Nobody is worth it. If somebody hurts or threatens you, or tries to come between you and your friends and family, leave immediately. Isolation from your friends and family is one of the abuser's most important tools. If someone uses it on you, get help and leave. Be careful leaving, abusers don't like to lose their victims. Keep written records of any abuse, but keep those records well hidden. Talk to doctors, your friends, your pastor and tell the police, but go! I was different, I never saw it coming, I had no idea there was a crazy stalker out there, but most victims of domestic violence do know. They know where the danger is and who's behind it, but for some reason they think the abuser will never really hurt them. He does. He escalates. Or she. Get help. Protect yourself and your loved ones. That's all I can say. God bless you all."

Again the onlookers in the studio erupted in applause, many of them had tears streaming down their faces.

Troy walked over to enfold her in a hug and give her a tender kiss. "Honey, I'm so proud of you. Your courage leaves me speechless. Let's go home."

Chapter Eight

"I will even betroth thee unto me in forever; yea, I will betroth thee unto me in righteousness, and in judgment, and in loving kindness, and in mercies. I will even betroth thee unto me in faithfulness; and thou shalt know the Lord."

(Hosea 2:19-20)

Once they decided to get married, neither Troy nor Nicole wanted a long courtship. They wanted to get married as soon as they could plan a simple but touching ceremony. They decided to get married at the ranch in a ceremony that closely matched the one David had when he married Emily.

That wedding had been extremely rushed, but didn't look it. Emily's father, Pete, who had cancer, had been very close to death. David and Emily both wanted him there, so they called on the members of both David's and Emily's churches to make it happen. The women from both churches made the food. They had dozens of casseroles and side dishes. The ladies cleaned the house until it was almost sterile enough for surgery. One of the church ladies was a baker and made a spectacular cake. The pastors of both churches shared officiating duties. Best of all, Emily's father managed to walk her down the aisle before sitting in a wheelchair for the rest of the ceremony. He passed away within days, but he was there for his baby girl's special day. Emily treasured that memory. She looked through the wedding album often and watched the video.

Troy and Nicole drew on that experience for their wedding. They reversed the usual order of things and sent out invitations before the details were actually worked out. They put out notices through both churches, and David invited people from his and

Nicole's client lists. Since he specialized in entertainment law, focusing on models, most of his clients knew Nicole.

Troy invited some old friends, his co-workers, and his parents. His mom and dad were surprised at the news, but they sounded delighted on the phone. Since they lived in Nashville, they would travel out a few days before the wedding and stay at the house that bordered on the ranch. Julia owned that house, although she kept threatening to put it on the market. She was a widow, with children who had grown and moved away. She simply did not need a large house and the five acres it sat on. David bought most of her land but Julia kept the house. She talked about selling it, but kept it without really knowing why. It was coming in useful for the wedding. Troy walked through it and had it professionally cleaned, and stocked the refrigerator. Then he made an offer on the house and bought it as a surprise for Nicole.

They would use David's large living room for the ceremony and have the wedding reception outdoors. Nicole had modeled hundreds of wedding dresses during her career so it was easy for her to find a dress that she loved. Since she knew most of the designers, it was also easy for her to get the dress tailored to fit her perfectly. She chose a dress that flowed out from her waist, the top had a sweetheart neckline under a lace top. The lace hid most of her scars at the neck, however her facial scars would show when she raised her veil. The scars ran mostly down one side of her face. She joked about getting a mask a la Phantom of the Opera, but in truth, they hardly bothered her. Troy would wear a dark suit that fit him perfectly and still managed to show off his athletic build.

They hired the same baker who had done the cake for David and Emily's wedding to make an elaborate cake covered in edible flowers and found a caterer to make the meal for the reception. They hired a pair of bartenders for a non-alcoholic bar, serving virgin cocktails, sodas, and soft drinks. One of them would specialize in milkshakes for the kids since so many of their friends had large families. They found a great DJ, one they both liked.

The only part that bothered Nicole was hiring a photographer and videographer for the pictures, and the right people for her hair and make-up. It reminded her of her friends who had been murdered because they would've been the ones to do these things. Ivan would work his magic on her hair. Lacey would create a make-up style to highlight her cheeks and eyes and Hans would shoot a wedding album that captured every moment in stunning beauty. He would find a great videographer to memorialize the wedding. She would always miss them, but planning the wedding made her miss them even more.

They wanted to have the wedding fairly soon because of her pregnancy. They wanted to be sure they were married well before the babies were born, and her doctor expected the twins to come early. So with the invitations already out, as soon as these arrangements were made they were ready for the big day.

Troy's parents arrived a few days before the wedding and stayed at the house Troy had just bought. They were an active, good looking couple, both in their late fifties. They got along great with Nicole's family, even Mae. They fell instantly in love with Nicole and told Troy how lucky he was.

Finally the wedding day arrived. It turned out to be a beautiful ceremony. Bonnie, Nicole's mother, looked spectacular in her mother of the bride outfit, a sky blue A-line dress with a beaded bodice. Troy's mother was chic in pale yellow silk. David gave the bride away with Emily acting as matron of honor, and Kate and Laura as attendants. Kate's twin daughters acted as flower girls, as they had when Kate, a widow, married their new dad. As they had at that wedding, instead of strewing the flower petals on the ground, they threw them at the guests. While the guests were laughing at the girls, Kate's son carried in the rings on a silk pillow.

"We should go into wedding planning," Laura whispered,

waiting to walk down the aisle. "Your kids are getting so good at it, and by the time they're too old you'll probably have more, and of course, there's always mine."

"And we're so good at matchmaking, we'll always have customers," Laura agreed, laughing.

The matron of honor and attendants began to walk down the aisle. They wore peach gowns, with halter tops and sequins. Emily's gown, as matron of honor was just a shade darker. Their husbands acted as groomsmen. The stairs and great room were draped in flowers, and candles burned softly on the counters and hearth.

The day was perfect and filled with love. There were a few refusals to the wedding invitations; most came from models who thought that Nicole was forgetting Lacey, Ivan, and Hans. However their families all attended, happy for Nicole, but still missing their own loved ones. During the ceremony, at Nicole's suggestion, one of the pastors made a point of mentioning the three of them in a poignant tribute.

Shelby covered the ceremony as a reporter but she was also there as a friend. She wanted to show that there could be happiness after a tragedy.

Detective Reynolds was there holding hands with Dr. Sullivan and Detective Mollney was there with her husband, a dapper man of around sixty. Dr. Haskell was there also, with Tina on his arm.

The policemen were there to guard against the elusive attacker. Several of them were there with dates they met through Kate and Laura.

Nicole only laughed as she saw Kate and Laura talking to her mother.

Soon her mother came over with a handsome, older gentleman on her arm.

"Nicole, meet Sid," she gushed. "He's a friend of Kate's husband."

"Welcome to the family, Sid." Nicole smiled at the man.

"Nicole! We just met!" her mother protested.

Nicole took her mother aside. "You were introduced by Kate and Laura, they're matchmakers with astonishing success. You're doomed."

She noticed her mother looking at Sid with a calculating look in her eyes throughout the afternoon.

After the ceremony, the wedding party moved outside. The weather was clear and sunny and the guests were enthusiastic. They had tables and chairs set up around the yard. There were four main tables filled with food. They had put vegetarian lasagna and salads on one side, and side dishes and baked chicken breasts on another. They also had a carving station for prime rib. The third table held an array of desserts, and the last held the wedding cake. Wedding guests lined up for food, split between the first two tables. Off to one side was the bar where everything was non-alcoholic. One server kept the blender busy making milkshakes for the numerous kids running around, and the other bartender worked on virgin cocktails. The service at all stations was fast and cheerful. Soon everyone was seated and eating.

The DJ announced, "Ladies and Gentlemen, please welcome Mr. and Mrs. Troy Dixon!" as Nicole and Troy came outside to a scattering of cat calls and applause.

Troy and Nicole sat at the main table with her mother and his parents. Kate and Laura had a table nearby with their husbands and kids. Frank and Lanie were seated next to them with Cassie and Lanie's sister, Tina, and her date, Dr. Haskell. The dogs were locked in the dog run, but they would get treats, like everyone present.

Nicole whispered in Cassie's ear and the girl ran off. She let the three horses out into the arena. The wedding guests could watch them run and play, but they were far enough away so the dust was no problem.

As the food was consumed, the DJ started pumping up the music, going from slow and romantic to dance music. He did stop for a moment, for the first dance, *"I Love You Just the Way You Are."* Nicole and Troy danced, floating on air and ignoring the other guests.

Soon the cake was cut and Troy and Nicole fed each other a bite without smashing it into each other's faces. The garter was thrown and the bridal bouquet was scrambled for by at least a dozen women. Troy and Nicole cut out of the reception and went over to Julia's house. During the day, before the wedding, Troy's parents had moved into Nicole's old bedroom. Even though the house hadn't cleared escrow, the newlyweds would move into their new house.

The wedding night was a little strange. Due to Nicole's high risk pregnancy there would be no lovemaking, but they cuddled, talked, and even without the lovemaking their love grew deeper. Troy told her he had bought the house thinking they would want their own place but to still be close to David, and the horses.

"That's the most perfect thing anyone's ever done for me." Nicole was sincerely moved and kissed her new husband. "I love you so much."

"Not as much as I love you." He returned the kiss. "Not nearly as much."

Chapter Nine

"And thou shalt have joy and gladness; and many shall rejoice at his birth."
(Luke 1:14)

Despite the identification of Adam Hannan as the man who had attacked her and committed four murders, there was no immediate arrest. Her attacker had fled. There were leads and sightings of him in several places: Michigan, London, Turkey, Iraq, and even Mexico. Nicole felt the danger she was in as a constant presence surrounding her, but she pushed the presence of evil back with prayers. She recited "though I walk through the valley of the shadow of death I will fear no evil" as a mantra. Her terror grew along with the babies in her womb, and she kept pushing that terror back with faith.

Her family and Troy were a real blessing for her. They surrounded her with comfort and love. She knew she was protected, but well, pregnancy hormones and the pain of the past few months kept sneaking in and trying to rob her of any peace or comfort.

The police visited her often. One or the other of the two detectives, usually Detective Reynolds, would come out weekly and give her an update. She used his visits to find out how his burgeoning romance with Dr. Sullivan was progressing. Her gentle but probing questions were as subtle as a sledgehammer.

Subtle questions like: "Have you and Doctor Sullivan set your wedding date yet?"

Detective Reynolds would blush and stammer, but he welcomed the not so subtle questions and sly teasing because it was a relief for him to see Nicole relax just a bit.

Finally, one day, both detectives came together and they were wearing big grins on their faces.

"We've arrested him!" Detective Mollney said. "It's over!"

Nicole sank to her knees, tears streaming down her face as she prayed. "Thank you, Jesus."

She stood after the prayer and faced the detectives, hugging them she said, "Thank you, more than I can say."

"There could be a delay getting him back into the US, he was hiding in London," Detective Mollney told her. "And you know he'll fight extradition."

"That's okay, I can be patient now that he's in custody." She hugged both detectives again.

There was indeed a delay as Adam fought extradition. He knew he faced life in prison or even the death penalty if he was returned to the States. He still felt justified in raping a whore and believed he had done what was right by killing her companions. He still believed there were virgins waiting for him in paradise, but only if he died a martyr's death. Lethal injection, however, scared him.

Although legally it shouldn't have influenced the courts, it helped move things along that Nicole was so well known in England.

There was plenty to keep Nicole occupied while she waited for Adam's extradition and for the trial to start. She and Troy set up a nursery in their new house. Troy did the physical work and she directed him over and over again. She was getting some payback for all those tough workouts by being a slave driver. Of course, he knew exactly what she was doing.

Some of her friends gave her a baby shower filled with tacky games and beautiful presents. A couple of the models who had turned down her wedding invitation came to the baby shower.

One explained, "We're sorry, Nicole, it just seemed strange to us that you were getting married so soon after Hans, Lacey, Ivan and Melinda were murdered. Then we heard how you had them remembered at your wedding and we felt really bad that we had

Susan Kohler

misjudged you."

"That's no problem, I understand, you're here now!" Nicole hugged them both, laughing. "Although I hope you brought really great baby gifts to make up for it!"

"We did," one of the girls said, "and even better, you get to watch us *not* eat the cake."

Nicole only laughed.

It really did amuse Nicole to watch as the models were served large pieces of cake covered in frosting. They each ate a minuscule bite of the cake, about a tenth of a normal piece for most women, and drank water. One good thing, Nicole realized, she no longer had to diet so stringently. She would have to be careful not to balloon up to overweight, and she would work to lose the baby weight, but she no longer needed to be stick thin. What a relief! She thought.

After the shower, she had everything she could possibly need for the twins, and more.

Since the wedding, Nicole and Troy shared a bed but they had not made love yet. The advanced stage of her pregnancy, which was a high risk pregnancy due to the injuries she had sustained, and the emotional and physical stress of the attack still lingered with her so she and Troy cuddled up and slept together without consummating their marriage. Until her attacker was caught they were living at the ranch, but they were remodeling and redecorating the house Troy had bought. They decided to move into the other house once the danger was over.

Nicole had passed 30 weeks in her pregnancy, and her doctor felt that she would deliver the twins early. Still, she was hoping the twins would wait a few more weeks to be born. She warned Nicole to call her if there was any chance she was in labor since she wanted to do a C-section. One night Nicole woke with a backache that was so severe she couldn't get comfortable. As the night went on the pain seemed to get stronger and come in waves. Soon she couldn't deny it, she was in labor at 34 weeks, and she hadn't called the doctor.

She woke Troy and called her doctor before waking up David and Emily. She already had her bag packed for the hospital, so she and Troy just went out to the car and started the drive to the hospital. Her pains were coming about every five minutes, and about halfway to the hospital her water broke. After that, her pains started coming about every three minutes and became more intense.

As soon as she got to the emergency room entrance nurses came out with a wheelchair and wheeled her inside. Troy had already set up her admission by giving the insurance information in advance, but he still stopped at the admissions desk while they pulled up Nicole's chart. Then he watched the nurses wheel Nicole into an exam room. Troy followed and joined her there and they waited for the doctor. Her doctor came quickly, examined her, and said she was 7 centimeters.

"I wish I'd gone ahead and done a C-section, but you have progressed too far for that now, and I really think you can go ahead and deliver the twins vaginally," the doctor said. "It should take a few hours, but you'll see your twins soon."

"I can't wait to see them," Nicole said between contractions. "It seems like it's been a long time and I really want to hold them."

"I bet they're going to be the most beautiful babies ever born!" said Troy. "How can they help it?"

"I've got news for you, Troy, they're always the most beautiful babies ever born." Doctor Sullivan grinned. "But these should be stunning!"

"I've got a call in for two pediatricians who specialize in neonatal care to come and take care of the babies as they come out," the doctor told Nicole. "I'm sure they'll be here in plenty of time."

It was weird how time seemed to fly by in an instant, yet still drag on for hours. In about two hours Nicole was fully dilated and ready to push. They moved her into a delivery room that already had two clear bassinets on wheels ready for the new babies. The pediatricians and delivery room nurses were standing by. Troy held Nicole's hand and murmured encouraging words to her when the doctor told her to push.

Soon the first baby came out, it was the little girl and she was small, only about three and a half pounds, but she was beautiful. It took a few moments before she started to cry. Once she did, she proved to have well-developed lungs. She was followed shortly by her brother, who weighed in at four pounds and instantly started to cry. Nicole was only given a moment to see both babies before they were taken away to neonatal intensive care. Both babies seemed to be healthy in spite of their small size which was a miracle considering all the stress and danger she went through with her pregnancy.

They had already decided on names for the babies, Lacey Mae for the girl and Henry Ivan for the little boy. When Nicole was able to get up, a nurse wheeled her down the hall so that she could see the babies, and they were the most beautiful things she had ever seen. She sat there in the wheelchair with tears streaming down her cheeks. David, Emily and her mom came up behind her. They stood there for a long time, saying a prayer of thanksgiving.

Once she got back to her room, Pastor Mark and Rachel came to visit. They'd gone to see the babies first, and prayed over them before visiting Nicole and praying over her.

Rachel hugged Nicole with a wide grin. "This is sure a better reason for you to be in the hospital than last time!"

Nicole was able to go home from the hospital in three days, but both of the babies stayed for a couple of weeks, growing bigger and stronger every day. Nicole and Troy visited often, along with Nicole's mother, David and Emily, Pastor Mark and Rachel, and the rest of the gang.

Nicole was healed from the attack and healing nicely from

childbirth before she began to remember the details of the attack. She began to have nightmares that seemed to be too realistic to be just regular dreams. During the day, details from that horrific day began to become clearer to her.

She saw her friends sitting around the table laughing. They were drinking coffee and eating the pastries sitting on a tray. She saw the photographer's assistant, Adam, hanging back off to one side, never really joining in the group. She sat to one side away from everybody to gather her concentration and to make sure that she didn't soil the garments she was supposed to wear for the shoot.

She remembered turning her head when she heard a thump and seeing Lacey on the floor. Hans was leaning against the table, almost looking drunk and Ivan was nowhere to be seen. She heard a sound behind her, and before she could turn to look she felt the blow to the back of her head.

She was not completely out, she felt herself being dragged across the floor and into another room. There was a funny smell in the air, at first she remembered it being the smell of a fire, but very faint. Now, as her memories grew, she realized it was the smell of gasoline and not a fire. The fire came later.

As her memories grew, she began to remember being beaten and attacked viciously. It was a long time before she remembered the actual rape, and it was horrible. As he raped her he called her names, degrading, horrible names and he was vicious to her in every way a man can be vicious to a woman.

She felt herself lying on the floor, barely conscious as he left. That was when she smelled the flames, at first faint and growing stronger. She felt the spray of water, but she passed out, unaware that being dragged into the other room had saved her from the worst of the flames and saved her life. She never knew how close she had come to dying before the firemen rescued her and the ambulance hauled her off to the hospital. She had fleeting memories of the terrifying ride to the hospital. She remembered being wheeled into the burn unit.

She was very badly injured with second and third degree burns, some broken ribs, and a concussion. Those were the injuries from the fire, there was also bruising and damage throughout her body from the beating and rape.

She never knew until later just how fast her mother had gotten there, catching the first flight in from Florida. She didn't get to see her mother for almost a week. She thought she'd heard the sound of her brother's voice calling out for her in the emergency room, panicked and worried, but she learned later that it had taken him over a day to get there. It was her own panic and desire for his comfort that put his voice in her head.

Chapter Ten

"A faithful witness will not lie: but a false witness will utter lies."

(Proverbs 14:5)

It seemed like forever before the trial started, but it was only a matter of months. Nicole both dreaded and anticipated the proceedings. She wanted to testify about what had happened to her, more importantly, she needed to be the voice for her murdered friends. She had to stand up for herself, to regain the last of her confidence and self-respect. The problem with her coming testimony was that the painful memories of that day were spotty and indistinct. Luckily, the detectives had plenty of physical evidence to back up her memories.

Because she was a witness, she was not allowed in the courtroom during the trial. Troy and David had front row seats and told Nicole they would give her the details after she testified. One thing they told her was that Adam had no one to support him, no family and no friends.

The trial started with jury selection, which was hindered to some extent by the reaction of many of the prospective jurors to a Muslim man being tried for a violent attack on a Christian woman. While such things were common in Muslim countries, the idea of it occurring in America resulted in a great deal of anger. During the questioning of potential jurors, many people admitted to harboring a prejudice against Muslims. And then there were the opposite ones; the Muslims who were in the jury pool and held a prejudice against Christian women. The next problem they had in selecting a jury was determining which potential jurors were in favor of the death penalty. It seemed like forever before they were able to seat twelve jurors and three alternates. Because of the high profile nature of the case, the jury would be sequestered.

The trial began with the prosecutor, District Attorney Anthony Strongfield, making his opening arguments to the jury. The courtroom was packed, but some of the police who were present for crowd control had also been acting as bodyguards for Nicole, and they promised to make sure that Troy and David always had front row seats for the trial.

During his opening statement the District Attorney outlined the crimes the defendant was accused of committing. He described the murder of Nicole's manager and talked about the murder of the three people at the photo shoot. Then he went into details about Nicole's attack and how she was viciously raped and beaten. He explained to the jury that it was a miracle that she got out alive. He described the evidence against the defendant including fingerprints, blood samples, DNA, footprints, tire treads, witnesses and more. He also talked about Nicole's identification of the defendant.

The last thing he described, in his opening statement, was a history of similar crimes against women that the defendant had been accused of committing. The defense fought against letting this information in, claiming it was prejudicial, but they lost the motion because the evidence was determined to be part of a pattern of behavior. Despite the ruling, the defense did win a small victory since the amount of evidence and many of the details regarding his previous crimes were going to be very limited.

The defense Attorney, Aiza Maro, gave her opening statement. Most of her arguments consisted of accusing the prosecution of engaging in prejudice against Muslims. She wanted it to sound as if all of the events were a big misunderstanding. She accused Nicole of setting a trap for her client, and being behind the attack herself. Once the opening statements were done testimony could begin as the government presented its case.

The District Attorney first began with the forensic testimony. He started with autopsies of the three victims at the photo shoot and Melinda Jacobson, Nicole's manager. He presented testimony from Nicole's doctors. Then he began calling in crime scene analysts to testify regarding the physical evidence found at the scene. The defense attorney fought each piece of evidence, but made very little headway. The District Attorney brought in the building's owner, who said that Adam had rented the building for just a day, paying a large sum of money for the use of the space. He called witnesses who had seen the defendant in the area carrying in tables, chairs and what they thought was photographic equipment.

Finally, the day came for Nicole to testify, and facing him was one of her greatest desires and worst nightmares. As she walked into the courtroom there was a gasp. For many her scarred face was a shock, even for those who had seen the public service announcements. Seeing her in person made the incident seem more real, more awful. Nicole had chosen to wear a simple powder blue sheath, and had her hair pulled back in a loose chignon.

She looked directly at Adam, seeming calm but seething inside. She swore the oath and took her seat at the witness stand. She gave her name and it started.

The prosecutor asked her, "What was your professional name?"

"Nikki Silver," she replied.

"And what was your profession?" the prosecutor questioned.

"I was a fashion model. I did magazines, runway and commercials." Her voice was firm and clear.

"Are you still a working model?" he asked.

"No," Nicole replied calmly. "My scars ended my career."

"Whore!" Shouted the defendant, jumping up. "You are a slut!"

The judge banged his gavel and ordered the defense attorney to get his client under control. Adam sat down, staring unblinkingly at Nicole.

"Okay, let's take it from here." The prosecutor asked calmly, "Were you a whore?"

"No, I was a fashion model and," she turned to stare at Adam, "I was a virgin and you know it. How could I be a whore?"

"You enticed me!" he shouted, earning more censure from the judge.

"Did you entice him?" She was asked next.

"In fact, I hardly noticed him. To me, he was a photographer's assistant. Our entire interaction was when he came up to me and said the photographer was running late and offered me some pastries and coffee." She kept her eyes on Adam. "He seemed nice enough, but we barely talked."

"Did you have any of the coffee and pastries?" he asked.

"No, I had brought my own coffee, and I had already eaten breakfast," Nicole said calmly. "One of the truths about modeling is that we do have to watch our weight."

"Who else was there with you?" She was asked.

Nicole paused, swallowing a few times, before she answered, "Hans, my stylist and a good friend. He was one of the best people I know. Lacey was my make-up artist, and also a good friend. She had a baby girl who was just 3 months old at the time."

Nicole paused again, controlling the urge to sob. "And Ivan, my hairstylist, also a good friend. A lot of people think the model does it all, but we're a team. I'm just the part of the team that gets the attention."

"What happened next?"

"I heard a thud and turned my head to look."

"What did you see?" the prosecutor pressed.

"I'll never forget it. I saw Lacey lying on the ground, lying still."

"And next?"

"I felt something hit me on the head, hard, but I retained some conscious awareness. I felt myself being dragged across the floor, into another room."

"Did you notice anything else?"

"Yes. There was a chemical smell."

"And next?"

"I was badly beaten and raped, my hymen was torn to shreds and I was brutalized. I suffered a concussion during the beating," Nicole stated firmly.

Adam shouted, "She was a slut. She hadn't even been circumcised like a proper woman." Once again, he was told to be quiet or he would be removed from the courtroom. "Your court has no power over me, I refuse to recognize your so-called authority!"

He was removed from the courtroom kicking and shouting all the way.

"I object, Your Honor." His attorney stood and protested, "He has a right to be present during the trial."

"If your client doesn't learn to maintain courtroom dignity, he can watch on closed circuit TV," the judge said sternly. "It's his choice."

Nicole continued as if nothing had ever happened. "And then suddenly there was fire everywhere. I learned later that my friends were trapped and died." Tears flowed openly down her cheeks.

"How did you survive?" came the quiet question.

"Apparently, the one thing he hadn't counted on as he planned this attack was that the side room he dragged me into had a working smoke detector and sprinkler system. They were renovating the building and had started on that room. I was the lucky one, even if I was badly injured. My friends all died." She cried openly, tears running down her face.

She reached for a glass of water as she heard the prosecutor say, "No further questions, Your Honor."

Then it was time for the defense lawyer.

She got up, a woman of about 30 with brown hair covered by a headscarf, and sharp brown eyes. "Hello, Miss Silver, I am Aiza Maro, attorney for Adam Hannan."

"It's Silvan," Nicole said firmly.

"What?" The attorney's head came up.

"My name is Nicole Silvan, Silver was my modeling name." Nicole was firm.

"Oh? You felt a reason not to use your real name when you were working?" She sounded annoyed. "While you were enticing men to sin?"

"I used a professional name for my work, and I never enticed any man to sin," Nicole said with defiance.

"Why do you say that? Wasn't it your job to entice men?" the woman shot back.

"My job was to sell products, whether they were clothes, make-up, fragrances, jewelry, cars or whatever. I was a sales representative. Also, a real man has the character and self-respect to see a beautiful woman and not lose control of himself by committing rape and murder," Nicole said with some contempt. "Only a weak coward commits rape."

The defense attorney turned to face Adam, putting her back to Nicole in an effort to control her volatile client. She faced Adam as she asked, "So you consider yourself a beautiful woman?"

"Not anymore." Nicole was quiet, somber. "But I was once. It's how I made my living as a model. I know that beauty is only outward, it fades or it can be destroyed. I also know that inside, in my soul, I am still beautiful."

"Yet you are not religious?" the attorney sneered.

"On the contrary, I am very religious. I am a Christian." Nicole smiled softly. "My love of Jesus Christ is what makes me beautiful inside where it counts, it's why I was a virgin."

"You are a Christian. Does that not mean you hate Muslims?" the attorney accused.

"No, I do not hate anyone," Nicole explained patiently. "I hate what some people do in the name of Islam, but I do not hate Muslims. I know there are Muslims who work hard, raise their families and live decent lives. I would like to see them convert to Christianity because I believe that is the one way into heaven, but I do not hate them. I do hate what Adam did to me and to my friends, but I do not hate Adam."

"Yet you make these ridiculous charges against him, do you not?" she argued.

"The only thing I said about him, at first, was that he was the photographer's assistant, and I thought he was killed in the fire too. I actually mourned him," Nicole replied, staring at Adam.

"Then, who accused him?" Was the question.

"The police investigating the case determined that he was alive and a suspect. They tracked him down to where he was hiding in London."

"You had a concussion. Tell me, how much of your testimony is based on your own memories, and how much was fed to you by the police?" the attorney accused.

"Every word of my testimony was based on my own memories, observations and knowledge," she replied with strength and determination. "I gave the police information, I did not take information from them except for vague updates on tracking your client. The facts I testified to were mine."

"No further questions." The defense attorney sat down.

Since Nicole was still not allowed to attend the trial in case she was recalled, Troy and David went to the courthouse every day and kept her abreast of the developments. They were the ones who told her what Adam said when he got up to testify. The three sat around the kitchen table after dinner and they told her what was going on in the courtroom.

"He was vile," Troy said, getting up to get a cold drink. "He was spewing hatred and throwing wild accusations against you all over the courtroom."

"Hey, Troy. Please bring a soda, too," David said.

"He claimed it was his right to rape you, and that murdering your friends was justified because they were Christians and therefore infidels," David added with cold outrage. "He bragged about killing other women, all over the world. And he said that you should be executed for adultery and for your lack of honor, because he knew you were not a virgin."

"I felt sorry for his attorney, she couldn't keep him under control," Troy admitted. "He seemed to have nothing but disdain for her. I think she was hired just to show that he felt more open to women than we've realized, but I think it backfired on him. All he's shown is his intolerance and arrogance. I also think she's afraid of him and maybe of someone else, whoever is paying her legal fees. I think if she loses this case she may be in danger."

"I wondered about that." Nicole paused. "I couldn't figure out why someone who hated women so much would hire one to defend his life."

"He never admitted to committing the crime he's accused of, but he bragged about similar crimes he committed in other countries. I don't think the jury is going to have any problem convicting him," David said. "Anyway, closing arguments begin tomorrow and the judge said that you could come into the courtroom now that testimony is completed. Right now, I think his only hope is for his conviction to be overturned on appeal due to ineffective counsel."

Nicole went to court for closing arguments. She sat next to Troy and David and listened as the prosecuting attorney outlined the evidence against the defendant. It was very painful for her to listen to the details of the deaths of Hans, Ivan, and Lacey. And it was excruciating to listen to the evidence about her own brutalization, the beating and the rape, and hearing how she was left in a burning building to die.

Hearing it outlined in cold detail only heightened the terror and horror of her memories. She sat there and listened with tears flowing down her face, and Troy handed her some tissue. As she listened she struggled to gain control of herself and prayed for God's help. She didn't realize how bad things could get.

At least she didn't realize how bad things could get until the defense attorney began her closing arguments. In the defense arguments, everything Adam did was a made to sound logical. Not just logical, but necessary. And she herself was demonized as an evil woman who set out to entice innocent men into sin and dishonor. She almost seemed to call for Nicole to be stoned. According to her, Adam was blameless. There was something almost desperate in the defense attorney's presentation, and Nicole remembered the speculation between her, Troy, and David the night before that the defense attorney was under the control of somebody else, that she was being directed in what to say, and that she would be held accountable if she lost the case. She seemed out of her depth, confused, and scared. By the time she sat down, Nicole felt that his attorney had done Adam's case more harm than good.

Since the prosecution was allowed to give a rebuttal, they had the last word. This time instead of the cold facts they described the people who were injured and killed by Adam during this horrific attack. They listed the family members, including children, who were left behind. They described the good works that the people had been involved in, in their neighborhoods and communities. They talked about their churches, and how they were all involved in different churches in different ways but they still served the Lord in their own way. And then he talked about Nicole.

He described her generous nature, and how she was always ready to help someone. How she always volunteered for charity causes, how she worked with her church to feed the hungry, and of her work to help women build up their self-esteem and confidence so that they could live a more productive life and take better care of their families. He talked about her career, and how successful she was and how that career was destroyed. And then he told the court about how she had used what had happened to her to help other women. He told the court that Adam had robbed her of her virginity but not her decency that was something she had inside of her, always.

He finished by calling for the jury to find Adam Hannan guilty of four murders, arson, and the battery and rape, and attempted murder of Nicole Silvan.

The judge gave his instructions to the jury, telling them what they could and could not consider when reaching their decisions. He reminded them that they were sequestered and not supposed to discuss the case with anyone but jury members, and he reminded them that the only evidence they could discuss was evidence that was admitted into the court transcripts. They could not consider any outside evidence. He explained to them what each crime Adam was on trial for consisted of legally. He talked about what a hate crime was. Then the judge sent them out to the jury room, and the verdict watch began.

Troy tried to take Nicole to lunch, but it was a real hassle with reporters and even a few fans hounding her. They grabbed a sandwich at a nearby deli, sat at a corner booth and ate their lunch. That's when it got really bad. Nicole could tolerate the reporters buzzing around like crazed bees. She appreciated her fans, even though at that moment, she wished they would leave her alone. She could even understand the few detractors, the ones who felt that by modeling, she had opened herself up to freaks.

But when Adam's supporters came things got really bad. They shouted that she was a whore, that she had lost her honor and she should be the one on trial. They called for her to be charged for her crimes and included their opinion that she was the one responsible for the death of her friends.

Due to the conflict between her supporters and Adam's, she

was escorted out of the deli by the police who showed her to a quiet room in the courthouse.

The wait seemed like an eternity, but it was only about eight hours. A court official came into the room and told her the jury had reached a verdict.

The jury filed in, looking grim.

The judge asked for the foreman to read the verdict.

The foreman said, "We find the defendant guilty on all counts."

Adam stood and started to shout something but he was quickly cuffed and dragged from the courtroom.

Nicole felt an overwhelming sense of relief.

A few weeks later there was a second phase to the trial for sentencing. Nicole asked to make a statement.

"Your Honor, Ladies and Gentlemen of the jury, I'm one of Adam Hannan's victims, but I'm not the one he hurt the most. He robbed the world of four beautiful people, people I counted as close friends. I cannot speak for their families, but I can speak for myself. I was brutally attacked, beaten and raped by this man. He left me with permanent scars." Nicole paused. "Probably most of you think I want him to face the death penalty, but I don't. I want him to have a long life in prison. I hope and believe he can change, if he does he can still do great things, even in prison. That's my hope. I also believe in forgiveness, as a Christian. It's hard, but I have forgiven him. And there's one more reason I'm asking you to spare his life. Your Honor, may I speak to the jury without Adam or his lawyer present? I have something very private and personal to say."

She knew the answer, even as she waited for the judge to deny her request. "Whatever you have to say, you will say in this courtroom, I can clear out bystanders but not the defendant or his attorney."

"There is one more reason I would not want to have Adam given the death penalty." She paused to gather herself, visibly shaken. "Adam doesn't know about this, and I hate telling him but... I don't want to have to tell his children someday that their father was executed for murder."

"Liar!" Adam screamed. "I have no children!"

Nicole faced him directly. "Adam, you have twins. A boy and a girl, born from rape and murder, but they are your children. They will be raised in love, not hate, and in Christianity, not Islam."

Adam was too shocked to speak.

Chapter Eleven

"By which also he went and preached unto the spirits in prison"

(1 Peter 3:19)

It took a lot of soul searching and prayer for Nicole to decide to go to the prison to visit Adam. After all, her new life was terrific. She had a wonderful husband she loved dearly, beautiful twin babies, and she suspected she had another one coming, this time conceived with love instead of pain and fear. She and Troy had moved into the new house, still close to David but with some privacy. Her mother seemed to be in a new relationship with Sid. She had returned to Florida but he had followed her. She emailed Nicole that he took her dining and dancing almost nightly. His energy level and adventurous spirit matched hers perfectly. Nicole's public service announcements were really helping people. She had completed her studies to become a licensed physical therapist, although she needed to intern and test for her license; and her new gym was opening in a few weeks.

The advertisements for the gym had been sent to doctors whose specialties would seem to call for physical therapy and weight control. Despite this weight control was not sold as the primary goal, health was, but it was treated as a side benefit of being healthier. Everyone on her newly hired staff was trained and instructed not to do or say anything that might lower a woman's self-confidence. More ads were sent to women's shelters with discounts for women who needed the help. Finally, just before opening day the ads were blasted over TV, radio, and in print ads.

The grand opening of Ladies Unlimited was a huge success. Nicole realized that some people came simply out of curiosity and a desire to see her. Still, they signed up to capacity. She had the finest equipment and staff available. The first thing she did with every client was to screen them for health problems and require doctor's notes before beginning any program. Then she set up an opening make-over with hair and make-up, wardrobe and professional pictures. She gave each new member a binder with room for monthly photos. The first make-over already boosted some of the women's confidence. She had dietitians and nutritionists help out with women who wanted the help.

Still, she felt something was missing. There was something more she was being called to do.

She and Troy talked about it for a long time and it felt as if she was being called on to visit Adam. It seemed like the right thing to do but there were some things she had to take care of first.

Nicole visited with the families of Melinda, Hans, Lacey, and Ivan. She wanted to explain that even though she would go and visit Adam this did not mean she was not forgetting their loved ones. In fact, she felt that she was honoring them by visiting Adam. She wanted Adam to know what he had cost the world. Moreover, she wanted him to feel the sorrow he had caused. She wanted to go with Pastor Mark on his regular prison visits, hoping that she could cause a change in the lives of some of the men in the prison by bringing her story and sharing her faith with them.

Pastor Mark discussed this with the prison superintendent and got permission for her to meet with men in small groups along with him. She didn't want to meet with Adam in a group setting at first, instead, she wanted to meet him alone, separated by glass. She had to admit to herself that despite his incarceration she was still terrified of him. In spite of this, she gathered her courage and went to visit him with Troy by her side.

The first meetings with Adam were conducted in a small booth with a glass pane between them. They had to use a telephone mounted on the wall to talk to each other. Adam was foul and virulent towards Nicole, swearing and calling her awful names while accusing her of being the reason he was in prison.

"You're right," Nicole told him with a deceptive calm, "I am the reason you're in prison. I'm proud of that. It was entirely your choice to end up here, for the rest of your life. Was it worth it?"

"Yes, I am proud of what I did to you and your evil friends!" he shouted.

"You're in prison because of what you did to me and my decent friends. You're in prison because you're an evil man who follows a belief rooted in hatred and violence. You follow a belief that women have no value and are there for you to use and abuse anyway you want. Then you blame them instead of accepting responsibility for your own actions. I was the one who survived and identified you to the police, so yes, I put you in prison, but your actions are the reason I had to do it. My friends deserved justice, and their families deserved to know that you were not going to be able to hurt anyone else. And I deserve justice, for the attack and rape and the loss of my innocence, even the loss of my career. You hurt me in ways you cannot even begin to comprehend."

"And I'm proud of it, you slut," Adam sneered. "You should be stoned."

"First, how am I a slut? Except for you, I would still be a virgin. Also, in my Bible, there is a story of a woman who was going to be stoned by a group of men who said she was an adulterer. They brought her before Jesus and asked him what they should do. His answer was: **He that is without sin among you, let him first cast a stone at her.** It's found in **John 8:7**. So for me to be stoned, even if I were as bad as you think I am, the man throwing the first stone would have to have never done anything wrong. He'd have to be perfect and perfect men do not exist, except Jesus. All men sin in one way or another."

For months their visits followed this same pattern, Nicole's quiet but strong condemnation of his actions followed by his verbal attacks on her. She made it in to see him about twice a week. What Nicole didn't realize was that Adam actually enjoyed her visits. It gave him a sense of triumph to see his handiwork and besides, the visits broke up the boredom of his existence. She didn't know that he was kept in semi-isolation for his own protection. So her visits, in spite of how he reacted to her, were a bright spot in his otherwise dismal and lonely day.

Gradually, over several months, he began to really speak to her instead of just yelling insults and profanities. It was a very slow change, and at first neither Nicole nor Adam realized it was happening. He began trying to convert her to Islam. When she realized what was happening Nicole was thrilled. This was the opening she'd been waiting for because his willingness to freely discuss his faith meant she would now be able to attempt to convert him to Christianity.

On her next visit Nicole talked to him about forgiveness, and how Christ died to pay for our sins so that we were forgiven.

Nicole looked Adam straight in the eyes that day and asked him, "How would you feel if you were me? Is it possible for you to forget your hate and disdain and put yourself in my place, just for a moment? Your friends have been murdered, and then you are beaten and attacked, and degraded in every way possible. Then you are set on fire and left for dead. Would it be possible for you to forgive the person who did that to you?"

Adam had nothing to say. He merely looked at her without a word, but Nicole thought she could see a hint of sadness is in his eyes.

Eventually he spoke. "Forgiveness is the tool of the weak, revenge takes strength."

"You're wrong," Nicole replied calmly. "Forgiveness is not easy, it's almost impossible, at least for as great a wrong as you've done to me. It takes strength, and courage, and prayer. I've tried not to ever hurt another human being, at least not physically. When this first happened, killing you would have been very easy, wrong, but very easy. Killing you would have just lowered me to your level."

"I can forgive you because I believe it's what God wants me to do. My Lord Jesus, even as he hung on the cross, beaten and bloody, and dying, said to those around him, **Father, forgive them; for they know not what they do.** How can I do anything less?" Nicole asked him very seriously. "It's in the Bible, **Luke 23:34.**"

"And when Jesus taught us to pray, part of that prayer was, to forgive us our debts, as we forgive our debtors, so when we forgive someone who wrongs us, we are following God's example," she explained. "Jesus also said, **But I say unto you, Love your enemies, bless them that curse you, do good to them that hate you, and pray for them that despitefully use you, and persecute you; Matthew 5:44.** That's why I'm here, trying to do good for you."

She never knew that when he got back to his cell her words wouldn't leave his head.

It was on another of her visits to the prison that Nicole finally noticed a slight, but real change in Adam's attitude. Instead of his usual hateful insults, he seemed to welcome her visit. She thought this change was just for the distraction of having a visitor but it turned out to be much more, it was a crack in the wall of anger that surrounded him. For the first time he seemed to listen to her words and pay attention to the verses she read from the Bible.

That day, she had chosen one of her favorite verses to talk about: **"For God so loved the world that he gave his only begotten son that whatsoever believeth in Him, should not perish but have everlasting life." John 3:16.**

For Nicole, that verse was simple and easy to understand yet still conveyed the essence of Christianity. She contrasted Christ's sacrifice to the belief that many had, that the way to heaven or paradise was to kill others. She spoke of her belief that suicide bombers who wanted to kill others to earn a place in paradise were murderers. She explained how Christ's sacrifice was to save others, to give any who accepted his sacrifice as a gift of life, earned a place with Him in heaven.

Her persistent visits began to bear fruit as Adam had now gotten to the point where he was asking her several questions with a sincere desire to find out the answer. He wanted to know what Christians thought paradise was and how to get there.

"We're not real sure what heaven is like, except that it's filled with joy, and peace," she explained. "And no one's perfect happiness depends on killing others or exploiting virgins. We believe you must accept Christ as your Savior to get into heaven."

He also asked about Christ and the virgin birth. "An angel of God came to Mary, and told her she was blessed, chosen to bear his only begotten son, the Savior of mankind. She was betrothed, but single. Her fiancé was visited by an angel, so he believed her and stood by her. They were traveling when her time came and she gave birth in a stable. The angels sang for joy, and shepherds kneeled in wonder," Nicole explained. "Of course, that's the short version. When you're ready to learn more about it, I can go into more details."

"I see," he said slowly. "But I do not understand."

"What didn't you understand, Adam?" she asked with a faint stirring of hope.

"Why didn't the Lord, as you call him, come into more, more um, comfort, a more prestigious family, an easier life?" he asked.

"He was not coming to impress men, but to save them. He was the Lord for everyone, not just the rich," Nicole explained, reaching, since she had never really thought about that particular point. "And I think, it was easier for him to be free to travel and preach. Of course, He was also fulfilling prophecy about his birth and humble beginnings."

"Nicole," he asked hesitantly, using her name for the first time, "do you have pictures of my son? I would like to see his picture."

To Nicole it was like a slap in the face. It told her his slight change in attitude was either an act, or it was really shallow. He asked to see his son, and never mentioned his daughter. Women were still less than human to him.

"No," she managed sadly. "I didn't bring any pictures."

"Maybe next time," Adam said to her, speaking calmly but clearly disappointed. "You could even bring me some verses from your Bible so I can begin to read them."

It was the first time he had responded at all to her Christian teachings. It changed her disappointment into hope. Nicole felt filled with joy. Was she really reaching him? She left the visit very encouraged. She told him once again that she forgave him for what he had done, the beating, the rape, and the fire, even for the death of her friends. She explained that for him to truly be forgiven by God, he would have to accept Jesus Christ as his Savior and ask to be forgiven for what he had done.

He wasn't ready at that time to take that step but at least he listened and thought.

Chapter Twelve

"Bring my soul out of prison, that I may praise thy name; the righteous shall compass me about; for thou shalt deal bountifully with me."
(Psalm 142:7)

Nicole started preparing topics to discuss during her visits with Adam. She secretly thought of them as lesson plans. She didn't realize how much she learned herself while preparing these lessons.

On one visit she spoke to him about the verse: **A new commandment I give unto you, that ye love one another; as I have loved to you, that ye also love one another. John 13:34**

She read that verse to him, and then asked him, "What kind of God wants people who will kill without mercy to get into paradise? Or heaven? Do you really want to spend eternity in paradise with people who are wanton killers?"

After a pause she added, bitterly, "Of course, you would fit right in, since you are a wanton killer and a rapist."

"I thought you said you had forgiven me," Adam taunted. "You sound bitter and angry, Christian woman."

"I have forgiven you, but that doesn't change what you are or what you did. I will never forget what you did, to my friends and to me. Sometimes the anger comes back. I'm not perfect, but I will pray and ask for God's help, and I will forgive you once again. I even pray for you," she shot back.

Adam couldn't have been more shocked at her rebuttal, his eyes bulged out, and he opened and closed his mouth so many times he reminded Nicole of a codfish. "What did you say, woman?"

"I said I pray for you, man!" She stood, even as she held the phone receiver up wanting to smash him in the face with it. "God knows you need my prayers, since you're such a monster!"

"How dare you address me like that! Man! I have a name and you will address me with respect!" Adam shouted to her.

And the fight was on!

"Respect? I have no respect for you!" Nicole was blazing. "You are a murderer, a rapist, and an arsonist! What is there for me to respect?"

"I am a man and you are only a woman!" Adam shouted back. "You have no value!"

"Women have as much value as a man, maybe more." She ignored his gasp of outrage. "No man alive could go through childbirth. And you! You are evil! You are the lowest, most vile form of evil on this planet." She released an anger she had endeavored to restrain ever since the attack. Her efforts at calm and control while facing Adam were shattered, and it felt glorious. "I have no respect for you, and none for any person who murders innocent people. Talk about worthless, you are a waste of food and oxygen."

"I did what I had to do because you have no honor!" Adam shouted back.

"And Allah decided you were the one to judge me? What honor do you have?" she shot back. "I was a virgin, and you know it."

"You go around with your head uncovered, and pose for lewd pictures!" he argued.

"I never posed nude, or lewd." She calmed slightly as she realized this argument could bring on a more open dialogue between the two. "I think the reason Muslim men insist on covering their women up, forcing them into arranged marriages, and even cause them to undergo female genital mutilation is that they are cowards, who fear that they cannot control a woman who has a choice. I think you are a coward."

"A coward?" Adam shouted back at her. "Would a coward do

what I have done?"

"Yes! Exactly!" She stood and looked him in the eye, this time her voice was cold and steady. "I think a coward would do exactly what you did to me. I pity you. You took away my choice of who I would give myself to. Women deserve to have that choice. You are a handsome man on the outside, but so ugly on the inside. Men like you know no woman wants a man with your attitude, so they try to control their women by fear and murder. Even a rumor about a woman can lead to a so-called honor killing. It doesn't matter if it's true or not. I pity men like you because they'll never know the true love or joy from a woman. You will never know true love or joy unless-"

"Unless what?" Adam sneered. "How can I know true love and joy?"

Nicole felt her heart thump as she realized the opening Adam had dropped into her lap. She silently and quickly prayed for help with her words. Dear Lord, don't let me lose this chance.

"There is a perfect love waiting for you to accept it," Nicole began. "The love Jesus has for you, whether you accept Him or not, His love is real and freely offered."

"But I have Allah and the prophet, why would I need Jesus?" Adam asked, amazed. "What good could your Jesus do for me? I'm in prison for the rest of my life."

"You have a choice, even now," she told him, sitting down again. "You can waste whatever life you have left, sitting in your cell and feeling hatred towards the rest of the world, blaming the world for your own actions, or you can accept Jesus and study the Bible. You can learn ways to help others, even in here. There is always some good you can do in this world, if you want to. Jesus will show you ways to help others. Like the Bible verse I read to you, Jesus commands us to love one another as He loved us."

Suddenly, Adam's mood turned. Nicole saw it come into his eyes even before he spoke.

"Allah is merciful," Adam said defiantly.

"You say that. I've heard it many times from many who follow Islam, but where is the mercy?" Nicole shot back. "Is there mercy in beheading a mere child? Or a man with his hands tied behind him? Is there mercy in selling a woman into slavery? Is there mercy in crucifying a man whose only crime is being a Christian? Does Allah really want people with him in paradise who only believe in him out of blood lust or those who fear for their lives? That's weak."

"You see, in my religion, there is free will. People have a choice to follow God and his son Jesus, or to reject him. God wants us to follow him out of love, and not out of fear. We don't kill you if you leave the church, we pray for you. Jesus died to save us, not to condemn us. We are taught that although the wages for sin is death, that Jesus paid those wages for us, if we accept him and repent."

"Doesn't that mean that you can sin and then just say you're sorry and all is forgiven?" Adam asked.

"In a way it does, but there's much more to it. We are expected to try to live a godly life, to do our best. We should try to avoid sin. But it's not because of the rules, not because of fear or cruel punishments. It's because we love God and we've accepted Jesus." Nicole chose her words carefully. "Also, once we accept Jesus into our hearts, we become changed and filled with the Holy Spirit. We have a desire not to sin anymore. We want to please God, every day, in every way. Still, we are human and we sometimes fail to do what is right. Heck, we often fail to do what is right, but we try because we want to please the Lord and we want to deserve the sacrifice he made for us. It's not easy, but we do what we can out of love and faith, not fear."

"So you do not pay for your sins?" Adam asked.

"Yes, we do," Nicole answered. "We pay according to man's law, and public opinion. We also face God's judgment. Jesus helped us defeat death, but we are still judged, in heaven. We still stand before the Lord."

"How did you defeat death?" Adam asked. "You still die."

"Yes, but we go to heaven." Nicole smiled.

"We go to paradise," he replied.

"Some paradise, filled with bloodthirsty killers and reluctant virgins who probably hate you." Nicole's smile spread even wider. "I'll take heaven."

She stood and started to leave, then turned back. "Adam, I'm sorry I lost my temper." Then she questioned, "Will you at least think about the things I said?"

"Yes." Adam grudgingly gave his word, "I will."

Chapter Thirteen

"And it came to pass, that, as he was praying in a certain place, when he ceased, one of his disciples said unto him, Lord, teach us to pray, as John also taught his disciples."
(Luke 11:1)

Nicole spent the evening with her husband Troy, enjoying a meal sitting out on the porch. She told him how, for a brief moment, she had thought Adam was opening up to Jesus.

"I must have said something wrong," she moaned as she gathered up the dishes to take inside.

"No love." Troy followed with the last of the dishes. "If God wills it, you will find the words to open his heart. All you can do is your best."

"Still, there was a spark of interest." She sat the dishes on the counter, and began to rinse them while Troy loaded the rinsed ones into the dishwasher.

"Have you considered that for him to accept Jesus he'll also have to fully accept what he's done? He won't be able to hide from himself anymore." Troy added the detergent.

"Let's put it aside for now," Nicole suggested, pulling Troy closer for a kiss. "We can go over to David's for a ride and a swim."

They walked over to the barn at David's house and got out the horses. Nicole smiled to herself as she remembered giving David the large, gray gelding, Ted. He was perfect for David, who rode but wasn't fond of gymkhana. Ted was great on trails and rail work, and he was easy going and affectionate.

"We really gave each other great wedding gifts." She hugged Troy. "You gave me a house, and I gave you Ted."

"And twin babies," Troy added, "who are trying to start

walking. Imagine them getting all over the house. Hey, did you hear? Emily's pregnant again."

"At least she knows it this time." Emily had been one of those women who went through a whole pregnancy without knowing it, until she went into labor.

They rode for a while, but Nicole wasn't in the mood to run any events, even though barrels were set up. She hadn't said anything to Troy but she was secretly hoping she was pregnant again, and though she was genuinely happy for Emily, she felt a little let down. And since her injuries and pregnancy, Cassie had taken over riding gymkhana on Burgie, so Nicole just rode for pleasure, exercising him.

After their ride, they put the horses up, pulled on their suits and jumped into the pool for a quick swim. David and Emily were there swimming too. They sat by the poolside and had soft drinks, and chatted about Emily's pregnancy. Emily glowed with excitement. Their first baby, Pete, was just over two, and a real handful. She couldn't wait for the second to come along.

"How are the prison visits coming?" David asked.

"Up and down." Nicole took a large sip of her soda. "One day he shows signs of listening, of opening up and then bam! The door slams shut."

"Are the listening times increasing?" was his follow-up.

"Yes, they are," Nicole admitted with a smile.

"Then you're wearing him down, Nicole, you're winning." David grinned.

"You're right!" She smiled. "Thanks, David. I feel so much better that now I'm going to take my sexy husband and go home."

Nicole felt refreshed after a few days away from the prison, but she kept visiting Adam. Even she didn't fully understand why, but she felt compelled to go. She and Adam were slowly growing closer, they weren't friends, but they were less combative. They prayed together, read the Bible and just talked. The only thing she held back from him was pictures and news about her twins. Sometimes she felt guilty about it, as if she had not really forgiven him but something inside told her, not yet. So she waited.

For her next visit, they discussed how wives should act towards their husbands. She quoted the verse: **Wives, submit yourselves to your own husbands, as unto the Lord. Ephesians 5:22**

As she expected, Adam really perked up when he heard the verse. It fit right in with his beliefs.

"See!" he shouted. "Wives should be submissive, circumspect, and do what they're told!"

"Or you can beat them?" Nicole said, her smile deceptive. "Is that what you think? Just boss the little woman around, keep them submissive, and beat them if they don't act exactly like you want them to act?"

"Is that not what the Bible says?" he sneered. "You stupid woman, you just proved how right I am."

"Oh, did I?" Her voice was soft and silky, her smile modest, but cunning. "Then how about the verse a few lines down?"

"What verse?" He was wary.

"So men ought to love their wives as their own bodies. He that loveth his wife loveth himself. Ephesians 5:28. That's the verse that tells men to love their wives as their own bodies, as they love themselves. Would you beat yourself? Keep yourself prisoner in the home? Would you kill yourself for being unfaithful?"

"It's not the same!" Adam protested.

"Isn't it?" she challenged. "Be honest, isn't it?"

"Maybe, in some ways," Adam admitted. "I must think."

Together they read through the whole chapter, discussing it verse by verse, line by line, even word by word. Finally, worn out, Nicole had to leave.

"Adam, please read it over when I'm gone. Think about it,

pray about it. Then you'll know how you really feel. In your heart."

"But who do I pray to? God? Allah? Jesus?" Adam gave a rare smile. "Do I just pray: to whom it may concern? What do I do?"

"Try all three," Nicole suggested, smiling. "And see who answers."

"Would your Christian God listen to my prayers?" Adam asked.

"Yes." She struggled to hide her excitement.

"But how?" he asked. "How do I pray?"

She held her hand up to the glass and said, "Jesus taught his disciples this prayer: **After this manner therefore pray ye: Our Father which art in heaven, Hallowed be thy name. Thy kingdom come. Thy will be done, in earth as it is in heaven. Give us this day our daily bread. And forgive us our debts as we forgive our debtors. And lead us not into temptation, but deliver us from evil: For thine is the kingdom, and the power, and the glory, forever. Amen. Matthew 6:9-13.** We call it the Lord's Prayer."

She left him there, thinking, and went home to her husband. She had a stop to make on the way first. She had a doctor's appointment.

Nicole was busy again, working on the anti-violence campaign, studying for her credentials in physical therapy, and getting her new gym off the ground. Surprisingly, she even had a few modeling jobs. With the right make-up, draping her hair in a certain way and the good old fashioned airbrush, she could look almost as good as she did before. Her saving grace was her experience and professionalism. With all that, and the prison visit on her plate, she was tired and a little run down. So she was shocked, thrilled but shocked, when she left Doctor Sullivan's office.

She drove home, feeling stunned. She waited for Troy to get home, and filled her time by fixing him dinner.

She had spaghetti and meatballs, garlic bread, and salads waiting for him as she heard the car drive up. She waited for him to walk into the house before turning to him with a big smile.

"I'm pregnant!" She leapt into his arms.

Dinner had to be reheated after they celebrated.

Later, she remembered to tell Troy that Adam had asked her to teach him a prayer.

"What a day!" He kissed her. "It's a miracle, you're making real progress with him, I know. And starting a new business, doing public service announcements, and now this! Nick, my love, we're having another baby!"

"You know the difference between you and Adam?" She kissed him. "He would say we're having a baby, and not even think about the two we already have. You know what? He keeps asking to see pictures of his son! His son! What about his daughter?"

"The sad thing is, to me, they're my kids." He held her.

"To me they are too, never doubt that. Thank God." She kissed him gently, with love.

Chapter Fourteen

"Moreover as for me, God forbid that I should sin against the Lord in ceasing to pray for you: but I will teach you the good and right way."

(1 Samuel 12:23)

The visits continued, usually twice a week. Sometimes she felt as if she wasn't making any progress, and while other times she sensed signs of a breakthrough, it was both frustrating and encouraging.

"Nicole," Adam greeted her on one visit, "do you always use the same words to pray?"

Nicole was surprised and pleased with the question. Partly because he seldom called her by name, and partly because he was starting to ask real questions. She had planned to discuss Christian views about helping others, but she decided in an instant to change that to a lesson on prayer.

"No, we pray from our hearts. We believe God is our Father, who listens and answers our prayers, but there are many ways to pray. This is my belief, so I'm not going to quote long verses to you. I brought you a Bible today, instead of just a few pamphlets, so you can read some verses."

"Here's what I've found for myself," she told him. "When you pray, pray without anger at anyone in your heart. Make sure you've forgiven anyone who has wronged you. That's part of why I had to forgive you. Pray for others, not just yourself. After you pray for something, you need to have faith and believe God will give you what you need. So thank Him. Do not wait for the thing you want to magically appear. Thank Him, and praise Him, whether you get it or not." She took a deep breath. "Sometimes God says no, but also sometimes there's something better in His plan for you. Also, if you pray for something, prepare to receive it. For example, if you pray for good crops, have baskets ready to put the crops in and a place to store them."

"But do Christians pray five times a day?" he asked, insistently.

"Most Christians pray many more times than that. I might say a prayer while I'm driving my car or before a meal, and of course, at church. I pray when I'm happy, sad, or troubled. I pray before I visit you. I talk to God to thank Him for my blessings. I can't tell you how often I pray."

"You ask God for things?" He was surprised. "And he answers?"

"Yes," she explained, "there are some great verses on prayer for you to read, for example: **And when thou prayest, thou shalt not be as the hypocrites are; for they love to pray standing in the synagogues and in the corners of the streets, that they may be seen of men. Verily I say unto you, they shall have their reward. But thou, when thou prayest, enter into thy closet, and when thou hast shut thy door, pray to thy Father which is in secret; and thy Father which seeth in secret shall reward thee openly. Matthew 6:5-6"**

She thumbed through her well-worn Bible. "We ask for what we need. God wants to give good things to his children. Just look what where tells us," she flipped pages then continued, "**Or what man is there of you, whom if his son ask bread, will he give him a stone? Or if he ask him a fish, will he give him a serpent? If ye then, being evil, know how to give good gifts unto your children, how much more shall your Father which is in heaven give good things to them that ask him? Matthew 7:9-11.** So if you pray, it's just between you and God. Pray, in the name of Jesus. I truly believe our heavenly Father can give you good things, even in here."

"What kind of good things?" Adam asked, glancing around at the glass cubicle. "What more is there left in my life?"

"I can't tell you exactly what God would like to do for you. He has a different plan for each of us," she admitted, "but you are a well-spoken, educated man. You can find a way to help other inmates get an education, you could learn to comfort the sick, even in here. You may one day become someone who spreads the word of God, and Christ, to other inmates."

"Me? Someone doing life for rape and murder? Your God would use me?" Adam was astonished, also intrigued.

Nicole smiled, what an opening! "Let me tell you about a man named Saul. He was a man who persecuted the early Christians, in fact we're told: **As for Saul, he made havoc of the church, entering into every house, and haling men and women committed them to prison. Acts 8:3.** And later we're told: **And Saul, breathing out threatenings and slaughter against the disciples of the Lord, went unto the high priest. Acts 9:1.** So Saul was one of the worst, persecuting and killing the early Christians everywhere he could find them. He went to Damascus to find Christians and take them bound, back to Jerusalem. But something happened to him on the way."

"What happened?" Adam was intrigued in spite of himself.

"On the way to Damascus, he saw a bright light from heaven and heard a voice. The voice said: **Saul, Saul, why persecutest thou me? Saul asked, Who art thou Lord? And was answered, I am Jesus whom thou persecutest: it is hard for thee to kick against the pricks. Acts 9:4-5.**" Nicole paused for a sip of water. "And then Saul was blind, and did not have anything to eat or drink for three days. A disciple named Ananias was told in a vision to go to Saul, and lay his hand on him to restore his sight. When his sight was restored, Saul rose and went to be baptized, and then began teaching about Jesus. People were stunned at the change in him. He was well known for persecuting the followers of Christ and now here he was, preaching about Christ!"

She smiled. "And what preaching, he was amazing! He

traveled all over, spreading the gospel. He was threatened, imprisoned, persecuted, and beaten. He changed his name to Paul, and he spread the word to Jews and Gentiles. He started several churches. Once, after being beaten and imprisoned, he converted the prison guard to Christianity."

She thumbed through her Bible. "And are you ready for this? In the Bible, the books of Romans, 1 Corinthians, 2 Corinthians, Galatians, Philippians, Colossians, 1 Thessalonians, 2 Thessalonians, Hebrews, 1 Timothy, 2 Timothy, Titus and Philemon are all letters Paul wrote to the early churches. So you see, God found a use for him."

"Before he was martyred for his faith in our Lord, Paul said: **For I am now ready to be offered, and the time of my departure is at hand. I have fought a good fight, I have finished my course, I have kept the faith, 2 Timothy 4:6-7.**" Nicole paused, tears in her eyes. "If He can use Saul, He can sure use you."

"I need to think about this," Adam said softly. "Will you come back tomorrow?"

"Yes, I will." She was overjoyed. He had never requested her to visit him before.

She placed her hand against the cool glass separating them. "Let us pray, and I will come back. Adam, would it be okay with you if I brought Pastor Mark with me?"

"That would be good," Adam agreed.

"Heavenly Father," Nicole prayed, "I've tried to help your child Adam, to show him your love. Please help him while he thinks about what we have talked about, give him your guidance, your love and your peace. I know he can do many good things with his life, even in this place. Show him a purpose. In Jesus' name, I pray. Amen."

She left, excited to get home and call Pastor Mark.

Once she got home, she had several things to take care of before she called her pastor. Real life intruded. She had to feed her children and play with them. She had to go out and feed the horses and clean their stalls. Then she started fixing dinner for her husband.

Once Troy came home she sat down to eat with him. Over dinner, she told him about her visit with Adam. He was cautious but optimistic, so they said a prayer before she called Pastor Mark.

Chapter Fifteen

"The time is fulfilled, and the kingdom of God is at hand: repent ye, and believe the gospel."
(Mark 1:15)

Nicole was excited as she called Pastor Mark that evening. She told him what she had said to Adam that day, and how he was thinking it over. She was almost positive he was ready to accept Christ. Pastor Mark agreed with her that it seemed encouraging, but he cautioned her not to get her hopes up.

"He may teeter on the brink, not quite ready to take that step. There is a lot for him to consider and I'm sure he has several concerns. There are lots of Muslims in prison, just as there are of any group or faith. The Muslims will see his conversion to Christianity as apostasy. Many of them believe that apostasy is punishable by death. If he converts to Christianity he will have a huge target on his back," he warned her. "Still, for his soul, accepting Christ is the best thing that could happen to him. I'll pray for him, of course, but it has to be his choice, and he has to be clear about it."

"I can't help feeling hopeful, but if I have to keep witnessing to him, I will," Nicole assured him.

"Are you still talking to him through a glass window?" the pastor asked.

"Yes, at first that was how I wanted it, but now I feel ready to be in the same room with him but the superintendent said I still had to visit through the glass. I'd like to be able to be in the same room with him, but so far, no."

"Let me talk to the superintendent and I'll come out and drive you to the prison tomorrow, okay?"

"Sure, thanks, Pastor." She hung up the phone.

She and Troy sat out on their porch and sipped lemonade.

"Want to go next door and swim?" he asked.

"Let's just relax here." She reached out for his hand.

As expected, Pastor Mark was as good as his word. When they arrived the next day, they were shown into a small visitor's room with tables and chairs but no glass. She was told she would have to sit opposite Adam without touching him, but for the first time she was allowed to be in the same room with him. Nicole admitted to herself that even after all these months, she was still a little nervous about the thought of being so close to him. She knew that he had changed, even without accepting Christ, but he had injured her on such a deep level that it was hard to let it drop completely.

Still, she was happy with the new arrangement, as much as she was glad for the comforting presence of Pastor Mark.

Her smile was real and warm as she greeted Adam. "How are you today, Adam?"

"I'm fine. Thank you for coming to see me again, Nicole," he smiled at her, "and Pastor Mark. How are you both?"

"We're both fine," the Pastor answered, "and very hopeful. Nicole said you were thinking about what she told you yesterday, about Saul and how he saw Jesus on the road to Damascus."

"Yes," Adam said slowly, "and how he became Paul, and wrote many chapters of the Bible. I read some of those verses last night. He was remarkable."

"We believe everyone can be remarkable, in some way, if they believe in Jesus. I pastor a church and minister to men in this prison, but I'm stunned by Nicole. Her faith and the love of Christ that she has in her heart is overwhelming. I could understand it if she hated you. I would try to have her forgive you, but I could understand it. Can you?"

"Honestly, if I were Nicole, I would be consumed by hatred."

"I'm not," Nicole spoke up, "and believe me, I'm no saint. It was hard for me to forgive you, but I did. Hating you would

119

consume me, that was a good way to put it. I would be filled with anger and hate and you would never have felt it. The hate would not hurt you, only me so I offered Jesus to you. He told us that if someone slaps you on one cheek, offer him the other. I had no other cheek to offer you so I offered you Jesus, instead."

"I wondered why you were so intent on witnessing to him," Pastor Mark said. "You went way past forgiving him, to the point of really caring for him. I find it amazing."

"So do I," Adam admitted.

"I'm not the important one here Adam, you are." Nicole met his eyes with a direct look. "Are you ready to accept Christ as your Lord and Savior?"

It seemed like forever before he answered in a firm but soft voice. "Yes, I am ready to accept Christ as my savior. I am ready to follow a God of love instead of hate, a God of forgiveness instead of judgment and revenge. I have been scared about making this decision because many of the Muslims in this prison will consider me guilty of apostasy, but I know in my heart that the dangers of converting to Christ are far less than the dangers of not converting."

He looked at Pastor Mark with a serious smile. "So, what do I do now?"

"First, we pray together." Pastor Mark grinned. "Then, we find out when we can baptize you."

"And we still meet with you to share our joy and worship," Nicole added.

"Guard," Pastor Mark called him over. "Can we hold his hands, while we pray as he accepts Christ?"

"Let me check." The guard moved away and spoke into his radio, before returning. "The superintendent approved."

"So let us pray." Pastor Mark reached out to grasp Adam's hands, and Nicole did the same. "Heavenly Father, today we are blessed. Our brother Adam has asked for Christ to come into his life. Adam, pray with me. Heavenly Father..."

Adam began to pray, repeating each phrase Pastor Mark said. "Heavenly Father, please come into my life. Let me know your son Jesus, and know that he died to pay for my sins. Let me feel the love of His sacrifice. I want to repent from my sins, and to be filled with His love. I want to learn to be more like Him, even knowing that I can never be perfect. I want to learn more and to try. Let Jesus, my Savior, who died for me, live in me forever. Amen."

As he prayed, Adam felt the power of the Lord move in him. Nicole, holding his hand, felt so moved that she had tears running down her face.

Pastor Mark finished his simple prayer and said, "First I want to teach you about the Holy Communion. Jesus knew he would be betrayed and arrested. He knew that the Passover feast would be his last meal, so during the meal he took the bread, broke it and told the disciples, 'Take eat, this is my body.' And he prayed with the cup and passed it around saying, 'This is my blood of the new testament, which is shed for many.' So to this day, we take communion, which is a minuscule bit of bread, and a sip of grape juice, but which is, for the sacrament, the blood and body of Jesus which was shed to pay for our sins. Do you understand?"

"Yes, I think I do," Adam said quietly.

"Would you like to take communion now?" Pastor Mark asked.

"Yes, very much," Adam replied. "Do you have what you need?"

Pastor Mark reached into his pocket and brought out some small pre-packed communion packets. He handed one to Nicole, one to Adam and kept one for himself.

"These aren't very elegant, but their meaning is the same, and that makes it very holy," Pastor Mark said.

He turned to the guard and asked, "Would you care to take communion with us?"

"Yes, Pastor. I'd be honored." The guard walked over.

The guard joined them at the table, and as Pastor Mark led the small group in a short prayer, they pulled back the plastic and ate the bit of bread that represented the body of Christ and sipped the juice that was his blood.

"What do I do next," Adam asked.

"The next step, when you're ready, is to be baptized," Pastor Mark said.

"What is that?" Adam asked.

"Baptism is a way to openly promise to be a Christian for the rest of your life. By baptism you declare your faith in Him, and you repent of your past sins. Jesus himself was baptized by John the Baptist. As he was baptized, according to the Bible: **And there came a voice from heaven saying, Thou art my beloved Son, in whom I am well pleased. Mark 1:11.**" Pastor Mark continued, "Jesus told Nicodemus: **Except a man be born of water and of the Spirit, he cannot enter into the kingdom of God. John 3:5.** So after you're baptized you can receive the Holy Spirit. What happens during baptism, is that the person who baptizes you immerses you in water and raises you back up to symbolize the end of your old life and your rebirth into a new life in Jesus."

"And then what's next?" Adam wondered.

"You read and study the Bible, pray, and you can join in our weekly Bible study and our Sunday services. Fellowship is an important part of being a Christian. In fact, we believe that whenever two or more Christians gather to worship, Jesus is there."

"That sounds good." Adam looked at Nicole. "Does this mean you will stop visiting me?"

"I will come as long as you want me to." She smiled at him then pointed to her belly. "I may miss a few days when she is born, but I will keep coming."

"You know this baby is a girl?" Adam asked.

"Yes, I had an ultrasound." She kept up the gentle rubbing.

"Is your husband happy," Adam asked, "or does he want a son?"

"We have a son," she replied simply, "and a daughter. This baby will already have a brother and sister."

"How are they?" Adam asked quietly.

"They are two now. They walk and stumble and talk gibberish. They keep me busy. I take them to work, and I have a nanny to help me with them." She said proudly, "Troy treats them as his own. I don't say that to hurt you, but I want you to know that they are loved and cared for."

"I'm glad. I know now how easy it would have been for you-"

"Don't even say it. I never could have, well, I did consider putting them up for adoption, but I felt them move inside me and I felt love." She smiled softly. "Just like I feel love for this one."

"She was amazing. She never wavered in her love for the twins," Pastor Mark said. "Now, back to you and your walk with Christ. We'll teach you something about worship. First, a good place to study in the Old Testament is Psalms and Proverbs. I especially love the **23rd Psalm**. Almost every Christian knows it well, it's simple and elegant. It says: **The Lord is my Shepard; I shall not want. He maketh me to lie down in green pastures: he leadeth me beside the still waters. He restoreth my soul: he leadeth me in the paths of righteousness for his name's sake. Yea, though I walk through the valley of the shadow of death, I will fear no evil: for thou art with me; thy rod and thy staff they comfort me. Thou preparest a table before me in the presence of mine enemies: thou anointest my head with oil; my cup runneth over: Surely goodness and mercy shall follow me all the days of my life: and I will dwell in the house of the Lord forever.**"

"That is beautiful," Adam admitted.

"And another verse we follow is: **Make a joyful noise unto God, all ye lands: Sing forth the honor of his name: make**

his praise glorious. Psalm 66:1-2. Many churches sing very old songs, very sedate and beautiful. Newer churches sing songs that are more like rock and roll, full of life and fun. I believe that if the words and spirit are right, either way is fine."

"Adam, when I come back, I'll bring some songs on tape," Nicole told him. "I'll even bring you some Christian movies. We enjoy our faith. I am so happy for you right now, but I have to get home."

"One thing, Nicole," Adam stopped her with his words. "When you visit next time, can I see pictures of my children?"

"I was hoping you would ask to see both of your children and not just your son. Your daughter is beautiful, and he's a good looking boy." She pulled some pictures out of her pocket and showed them to the guard before handing them to Adam. "You can keep these as a gift for you on the day you accepted Christ."

"Thank you, Nicole, for more than I can ever tell you." Adam had his own tears forming in his eyes.

On her next visit, Nicole learned that Pastor Mark had set up a baptism ceremony for Adam in the prison chapel. As she watched he prayed with Adam, and read a few verses from the Bible. He read: **"He said unto them, Have ye received the Holy Ghost since ye believed? And they said unto him, we have not so much as heard whether there be any Holy Ghost. And he said unto them, Unto what then were ye baptized? And they said unto John's baptism. Then said Paul, John verily baptized with the baptism of repentance, saying unto the people, that they should believe on him which should come after him, that is, on Jesus Christ. When they heard this, they were baptized in the name of the Lord Jesus. Acts 19:2-5."** Pastor Mark paused for a breath. "Let's pray.

Heavenly Father, we rejoice in this man's choice, of his free will to follow Christ, and to be baptized in His name. Bless him and keep him safe, let his faith grow, and help him find a new

purpose and meaning to his life, in Jesus name we pray."
With that simple prayer he baptized Adam.

Chapter Sixteen

"Now the end of the commandment is charity out of a pure heart, and of a good conscience, and of faith unfeigned."
(1 Timothy 1:5)

A few months after Adam's conversion, as Nicole's pregnancy advanced, she cut down her visits to once a week. Between her new business and the pregnancy it was just too hard on her to drive out to the prison. One day though, she was especially excited to go visit Adam. She had spent the previous afternoon at home on one of the rare days when she and Troy had the same afternoon off.

Cassie was over riding Burgie and getting him ready for a show next weekend. Since she had started showing him, she'd done very well winning lots of ribbons and several trophies. When she was done, she rinsed off Burgie and put him on the hotwalker. Troy was unsaddling Ted, but he hadn't ridden hard enough to make him sweaty. The twins were excited, talking gibberish and pointing at the horses. Nicole stood up and walked over to the saddling rack with them.

"I have an idea, Troy." She smiled up at him. "Let's give these two a ride. I can lead Ted and you can walk alongside and make sure no one falls off. Cassie would probably take the other side, just to be safe."

Cassie had walked over just in time to hear that. "I have a better idea. I can run up and get David to come out and videotape them riding."

"Great, Cassie, and bring some juice back with you," Nicole called after the girl's retreating back.

The twins took to sitting on the horse like ducks to water, ducks with a very careful mama duck watching. They bounced

126

and laughed on the gray gelding's back as he patiently plodded around the small round pen, little feet that could barely reach the horse's sides kicked wildly. David videotaped the ride, laughing as he filmed it. He already had a similar tape of Pete on his horse.

It wasn't long before they put the horse up and fed all four of them. They cleaned the stalls, but Nicole claimed she wasn't on stall cleaning duty until after the baby was born. The group left the barn and headed for the pool. After a few quick changes the whole group splashed around for a while. The twins loved the water. David again manned the video camera. Cassie left when her mom came. David went inside and Troy and Nicole went home.

On her next visit to Adam, she was excited. She showed him the video of the twins on the horse and in the pool. He laughed and smiled throughout the tape but there was a real sadness behind his smile. He was extremely glad she had brought him the video, but it really made his confinement hit home. They didn't do much Bible studying that day. They just watched the tape over and over, and she talked to him about the children. She did tell him about how Jesus reacted when people brought their children for him to bless. The disciples tried to keep the children away. **But when Jesus saw it, he was much displeased, and said unto them, "Suffer little children and forbid them not, to come unto me: for of such is the kingdom of heaven. Mark 10:14."**

A few days later she told him, "I want to talk to you about helping others. In Matthew, Christ talks to his disciples about helping people. For when I was an hungered, and ye gave me meat: I was thirsty, and ye gave me drink: I was a stranger, and ye took me in: Naked, and ye clothed me: I was sick, and ye visited me, I was in prison, and ye came to me. Matthew 25:35-36. And his disciples asked him when they had done these things, And the King shall answer and say unto them, Verily I say unto you, Inasmuch as ye have done it**

unto one of the least of these my brethren, ye have done it unto me. Matthew 25:40. And he told the ones who didn't help others in these ways, if they didn't help the least of these they didn't do it for him." She stopped and sipped her water.

"Is that why you visit me in prison?" Adam asked.

"It's part of the reason, another is for my sake. I cannot walk with God the way I want to if I don't forgive you," she admitted.

"I see."

"But there's more to helping than the man on the street, or me and you. When there's a natural disaster, like an earthquake or a flood, Christians go to give aid. Not just aid for other Christians but for everyone who needs it. And even when there is no disaster, just a need, there are Christian charities. Not just to spread the word of God, but to spread his love." Nicole smiled. "It can be dangerous, aid workers have been kidnapped, tortured and murdered in some countries and yet they still go. Jews do it too. We go out of faith and to show our love of Jesus. We donate food, money, clothes, building supplies and school books for children, mosquito nets, vaccines and even toys."

"All of that? Even toys?" Adam was surprised.

"Yes, toys are good for a child's spirit, to help them smile and be a kid." She smiled at Adam.

"There's another example of Jesus speaking of helping others, he said: **When thou maketh a dinner or a supper; call not thy friends, or thy brethren, neither thy kinsmen, nor thy rich neighbors; lest they also bid thee again and a recompense be made thee. But when thou maketh a feast, call the poor, the maimed, the lame, the blind: And thou shalt be blessed; for they cannot recompense thee: for thou shalt be recompensed at the resurrection of the just. Luke 14:12-14.**"

"Muslims have charities too," Adam told her.

"Yes, I know. I looked it up online. Most Muslims are just people trying to live their lives, like all of us," she admitted.

"Some of the charities funnel money to extremist groups, and some only give aid to Muslims, not to infidels in the area, but most are decent people trying to do good works. One big difference is we give aid and relief to everyone, even to people who are attacking us."

"Why?" Adam asked, surprised.

"We're told to," Nicole replied. "Jesus said, **But I say unto you which hear, Love your enemies, do good to them which hate you, Bless them that curse you, and pray for them which despitefully use you. Luke 6:27-28.** And a few verses down, He said: **For if ye love them which love you, what thank have ye? For sinners also love those that love them, and if ye do good to them which do good to you, what thank have ye? For sinners also do even the same. Luke 6:32-33.** And later still: **But love ye your enemies, and do good, and lend, hoping for nothing again; and your reward shall be great, and ye shall be the children of the Highest: for he is kind unto the unthankful and to the evil. Be ye therefore merciful, as your Father is also merciful. Luke 6:35-36.**"

"Jesus preached about love quite a lot, didn't he?" Adam commented.

"He often gave lessons in the form of parables, stories with a message. One of my favorites is the story of a man who was traveling when thieves robbed him, beat him, and left him by the side of the road almost dead."

"What happened to him?"

"Well, people came along, saw him, and walked on by on the other side of the road. Finally a Samaritan saw him and dressed his wounds, put him on his donkey, and took him to an inn. He gave the innkeeper some money to care for the man, and said if it wasn't enough he'd pay more on his return trip. Jesus used it to show how we should help others, and how those that passed by were not doing His will, but being selfish."

"Is that why you are so good to me?" Adam asked. "To earn your reward in heaven?"

"Partially, at first. I wanted to make sense out of what happened to me. It started small and grew, even before I liked you, I cared about your soul."

"Do you really like me now?" Adam was stunned.

"Yes," Nicole admitted, smiling. "I do."

He was speechless.

"Maybe that's why we're told to love our enemies, and to do good to someone who has harmed us." She thought as she spoke. "God wants us to live in peace and love, but it has to start somewhere, with someone willing to take on the hatred and face it with love. Jesus did more than preaching and speaking in parables. As he walked the land and taught the people he also performed many miracles."

"What miracles?" Adam asked.

"He calmed the storm and walked on water. He healed the sick, cast out devils and even raised the dead."

"Raised the dead?"

"There was a man named Lazarus who was a friend of Jesus. He died and it took Jesus four days to get to his family. Jesus spoke to his sister, Martha. **Jesus said unto her, I am the resurrection, and the life: he that believeth in me, though he were dead, yet shall he live: And whosoever liveth and believeth in me shall never die. Believeth thou this? John 11:25-26.** Martha said she believed so she and her sister Mary went with Jesus to the grave where Lazarus was buried. He called to Lazarus and told him to come out and Lazarus did. Another time when he was preaching the disciples wanted to send people home to eat. Jesus asked how much food they had, and the disciples said five loaves of bread and two fishes. Jesus blessed the food and began breaking it up. The whole group was fed, and there were twelves baskets of leftovers. Do you know how many were fed?"

Adam just said quietly, "No."

"Five thousand men and their wives and children."

"Amazing. Nicole, I want to ask you something." Adam hesitated. "Why did you go ahead and have my babies?"

"I've told other people who questioned me that I do not believe in abortion, and that's part of it. I also saw the pregnancy as a gift, something good coming from something bad. That was another part. I also did it for me, because I was afraid. Afraid that with these scars, I would never find a man to love me, to be my husband, and I would wind up alone. Those babies gave me hope for the future."

"Thank you," Adam said simply.

"You're welcome."

Chapter Seventeen

"And the disciples came, and said unto him, Why speakest thou unto them in parables?"
(Matthew 13:10)

A few days after Nicole had the discussion with Adam about the twins, she was lounging by the pool waiting for Troy to come home. She had just reached for her glass of lemonade when the first twinge hit. She noted the time and wondered if it was the start of labor or just a random pang. By the time Troy got home, she'd had more than four twinges, the last couple of them were about 10 minutes apart.

When Troy arrived she was ready. She had already put her bag in the car and talked to Emily and Julia about watching the twins.

He walked in and gave her a big kiss. "Hi, Sweetie." He kissed her again. "What have you been up to today?"

"Me?" All innocent, she smiled at him. "Just sitting here wondering."

"Wondering what?" He picked up her glass and sipped at her lemonade.

"Well, for one thing, I was wondering if you would get home before I had to go to the hospital. I'm in labor."

"Are you ready to go?" He smiled. "Packed? Kids taken care of? Doctor called?"

"Yes, my go bag is in the car, Emily and Julia are watching the twins, and I called Dr. Sullivan." She grinned. "So give me a hand getting up from this lounge and we can go."

"I can't wait to meet my new daughter." Troy's smile was huge.

On the drive to the hospital Nicole called Pastor Mark and asked him to tell Adam she wouldn't be in to see him for a while.

The pastor told her that Adam had finally begun coming to a prayer meeting group held every Wednesday in the prison. He was planning on coming to Sunday services, too. Mark told her the group was learning worship songs, and they were planning a few movie nights for the group.

Nicole was quickly admitted to the hospital and wheeled up to a room. That was the last quick thing that happened. Unlike her first pregnancy where labor and delivery was fast, even with twins, this was a long, slow process. Luck was with her however, she had plenty of time for an epidural. It took about six hours but she had her baby girl. Unlike her siblings, who were both under 4 pounds, baby Sarah Jean weighed in at 8 pounds 3 ounces. She was beautiful, healthy and prefect.

Nicole and Sarah stayed overnight at the hospital, of course the visitors descended en masse, Kate and Laura and their husbands, Lanie and Tina with Cassie, Pastor Mark and Rachel, David and Emily. The room was flooded with flowers, which Nicole gave away, and balloons.

Troy's face seemed to be stuck in a permanent smile.

They took Sarah home the next day. The twins, now about halfway through the terrible twos, were fascinated with the new addition, although Nicole kept an eagle eye on the pair. They were too good at mischief.

It was about two weeks before Nicole went back to the prison. Adam was glad to see her and asked to see more pictures of the twins, but to Nicole's surprise, he also asked to see pictures of Sarah. He took a long look at Sarah and pronounced her beautiful. That was more than he said about pictures of the twins. In the latest picture, they were playing in the straw in the barn, and they were both filthy, smiling, but filthy.

He laughed, looking at the pictures. "That's my children, covered in hay."

"And loving it," Nicole added. "They are good kids, Adam, even now in their terrible twos."

They chatted about the kids for a while before Adam turned the conversation to the prayer group.

"I really enjoy it," Adam said. "And I keep learning more every week."

"What's it like?" she asked, smiling. "What are you learning?"

"Well," he thought, "we've studied how the Old Testament and the New Testament fit together, and I've learned to enjoy worship. I've learned some worship songs and last week we saw a movie about a high school football team who followed Jesus. It was a great movie."

"Yes, I know the movie you mean. *Facing the Giants*, written, directed, and starring Alex Kendrick. The Kendrick brothers have a great talent. They could make a fortune with mainstream movies, but they choose to serve the Lord. Their movies have humor, a real feeling for life, sometimes sadness and problems, but they always show the greatness of God's love."

"We're seeing *The Passion of the Christ* next week."

"That's a very violent movie, it really shows what Christ went through for us. It's amazing. He did that willingly to pay for our sins."

"And later on we're seeing a movie called *Courageous*." He seemed to be looking forward to it.

"You'll love that movie." Her smile was warm. "That gives me an idea. One of the things you can do, even in here, is write. Paul wrote in prison. Why not you?"

"Me? Are you crazy?" He was shocked.

"Why not, write for yourself, even if it's not for anyone else. You're already keeping a journal from what I hear."

"Well, yes, I am," he admitted.

"So expand it," she told him. "I've got to get home."

She came back in a few days.

"What shall we talk about today?" Nicole asked him.

"You told me a little bit about parables. Can you tell me more?"

Nicole opened her Bible. "Sure, we can read and study some together."

She thumbed through the Bible, starting at Matthew. "Hmm, let's see... here's a good one, look at these verses, **Matthew 13:3-8.** You read them to me this time."

Adam read, **"Behold, a sower went forth to sow; And when he sowed, some seed fell by the wayside and the fowls came and devoured them up.** What does that mean?"

"This is my interpretation: The ground is people. Some hear the words of Christ but their hearts are hard and the word does not sink in, so the devil takes it away," she explained. "Continue."

"And some fell on stony places, where they had not much earth: and forthwith they sprung up because they had no deepness of earth: And when the sun was up, they were scorched; and because they had no root, they withered away. Let me guess, the stony earth represents people with no depth to them, who fall apart when there is trouble because there are no roots to their faith." Adam smiled widely. "Am I right?"

"Fantastic!" Nicole told him. "I am so proud of you."

"And some fell among thorns; and the thorns sprung up, and choked them: What are the thorns?"

"I think the thorns are the daily pressures of life," she said, thinking. "They can overwhelm you, and hide God from your view, cutting you off from Him."

"But the other fell into good ground, and brought forth fruit, some a hundredfold, some sixtyfold, some thirtyfold. Does that mean that people who hear the word and take it to heart spread the word to others and those others are the fruit they bear?"

"By George, I think you've got it!" She was thrilled, so happy tears started to form in her eyes.

"Let's do another," Adam suggested. "Do you have time?"

"Not much, I do have to go feed the baby, but I do have some time to spare. How about the parable of the lost sheep?

Jesus said: **What man of you, having a hundred sheep, if he loses one of them, doth not leave the ninety and nine in the wilderness, and go after that which is lost until he find it?** You finish it," Nicole suggested. "It's **Luke 15:4-7**, I left off at verse 4."

"**And when he hath found it, he layeth it on his shoulders, rejoicing, And when he cometh home, he calleth together his friends and neighbors, saying unto them, Rejoice with me; for I have found my sheep which was lost. I say unto you, that likewise joy shall be in heaven over one sinner that repenteth, more than over ninety and nine just persons that need no repentance.**" Adam said, "I am the lost sheep, am I not?"

"Yes, you should also read on down, the rest of the chapter. You will find the Parable of the Lost coin, and the Parable of the Lost Son. They both follow this topic. I have to go, I'll see you soon." She picked up her sweater and put it on.

"Adam," she said softly, "I am so glad you were found."

Chapter Eighteen

"Yea, and all that will live godly in Christ Jesus, shall suffer persecution."
(2 Timothy 3:12)

The next day, Nicole and her family had a large picnic. The whole gang was there, David and Emily with their two children, Pete who was getting old enough to be a handful to watch, and baby Grace. Mae and Julia were sitting at the patio table while David and Troy worked the barbecue grill. Kate and Laura brought their husbands and a whole passel of kids plus their Boston Terriers. Kate had a Boston which she'd bred twice and somehow all the puppies stayed with this group. The Bostons played with David's ranch dogs. Lanie and her husband Frank brought Cassie, their Boston, and even her horse.

The horses were saddled and all the kids rode with helmets on their heads. The older children rode by themselves, some of the younger children had a pair of adults walking alongside them, and a few rode while being held in an adult's arms. After riding and putting the horses up, the group changed into swimsuits and jumped in the pool. With two adults at all times assigned to do nothing but watch the children swimming it was safe, very loud and splashy, but safe.

The meal itself was a feast: potato salad, coleslaw, barbecue beef, hamburgers, salads, corn on the cob, french fries, and a lot of desserts, everything from homemade ice cream to apple pie and chocolate cake. By the time everything was eaten and the tables cleaned up, everyone including the adults needed a nap.

As she sat at the picnic table, Nicole talked with David and Troy.

"I'm getting to the point where I'm having trouble finding

topics to share with Adam," she told them. "I've talked about forgiveness, charity, some parables, Saul on the road to Damascus, and more. I know there's a lifetime of topics to study, no one ever knows it all, but what should I talk about next?"

"Have you gone through the Old Testament with him?" David asked.

"I've referred to it, but not in any detail." She sipped her iced tea. "His Bible study class has gone into the Old Testament more than I have. I felt like the verses and stories from the New Testament would help me more in my effort to introduce him to Jesus. And I think it worked, but what's next?"

"That's it!" Troy sat upright, excited. "Talk to him about what's next in prophesy and the end times."

"I hate to open that can of worms," Nicole admitted as she sipped more tea. "There's so much dispute about what's going to happen, even among Christians. You know, there is no rapture, the rapture will come before the tribulation or mid-tribulation, or even after. I need to do some research."

"Then do the research, but for now... try apostasy and persecution." David laughed at his sister's expression.

"God only knows what I'll find out." Nicole sighed.

"That's the point, isn't it?" Troy rubbed Nicole's shoulder. "You know what?"

"What?" she asked.

"You don't have to have all the answers, you can tell him you're not sure of some things. At first, to convert him, it was important for you to be on solid ground. Now you can explore with him and let him find his own answers."

Nicole leaned into his embrace. "Good point."

She was shocked when she went to see Adam a few days later. He had been beaten badly, his face was bruised and his wrist was wrapped. He moved slowly, and she learned one of his ribs was broken.

"Adam!" She was shocked. "What happened to you?"

"I was attacked," he muttered, his mouth was so swollen it hurt to speak. "The Muslims in here aren't too happy with me. My conversion to Christianity is apostasy, you know."

"I was afraid this would happen, I've heard many stories about how Muslims treat apostasy." Nicole thought as she thumbed through her Bible. **"Then Jesus said unto his disciples, if any man should come after me, let him deny himself, and take up his cross, and follow me. Matthew 16:24.** This tells us that as we follow Jesus we will also be persecuted for our beliefs. It will not always be easy, or even safe."

"I know," Adam admitted. "I persecuted Christians myself. Now I look back and feel as if it was someone else doing those things. I have so many regrets."

"You are not the same man you were." She smiled at him. "I know you've really changed. Remember when we discussed the Sermon on the Mount?" At his nod she continued, "One of the verses we call the Beatitudes says: **Blessed are ye, when men shall revile you, and persecute you, and shall say all manner of evil against you falsely, for my sake. Rejoice and be exceedingly glad: for so persecuted they the prophets which were before you. Matthew 5:11-12."**

"Well, I'm blessed today then, but it's a little hard to be exceedingly glad when my mouth hurts so much I can hardly talk." He grinned and winced. "But I do remember you reading me this verse: **But I say unto you, Love your enemies, do good to them that hate you, and pray for them which despitefully use you, and persecute you. Matthew 5:44.** You not only read that verse to me, you lived it for me. You've shown me nothing but love, forgiveness, and patience, Nicole, thank you."

"I've gotten so much back, you will never really know how much, but another thing you will never really know is how hard it was for me to come here, at first," she admitted. "It was this verse that helped me: **Bless them that persecute you, bless and curse not. Romans 12:14."**

"That's not always easy, is it?" Adam asked softly. "Even for you."

"No, it wasn't easy." She smiled at him. "But it was worth it. Since the attack, I've found a husband, a man I would have never met otherwise, I've had three beautiful children, started a new business, and found a way to help other abuse victims. Best of all, I've found a way to help you. I'm happy with my life."

"I'm glad." Adam was humbled.

"Some people claim that Christianity is a hoax. It was just a plot to promote a new religion," Nicole told him. "That seems outrageous to me. For that to be true hundreds, maybe thousands of people had to plan together to let themselves be imprisoned, tortured, and murdered in the most violent ways possible, not because of faith, but to promote a lie. Could you let yourself be burned alive or fed to the lions without renouncing your faith in Jesus? Who would do that?" Her voice rose a bit with agitation. "Would you agree to be tortured or killed for a lie? In the case of the first Christians, what would they gain? Nothing! They would be dead. It doesn't make sense."

"It seems wrong," Adam admitted.

"It happened to the earliest Christians, for example, Stephen was imprisoned and defending himself when he said: **Which of the prophets have not your fathers persecuted? And they have slain them which shewed before of coming of the Just One; of whom ye have been now the betrayers and murderers. Acts 7:52.** His accusers then stoned him to death. His last words were very much like the last words of Jesus."

"Father forgive them for they know not what they do." Adam remembered the quote.

"Yes, the Bible tells us: **And they stoned Stephen, calling upon God, and saying, Lord Jesus receive my spirit. And he kneeled down and cried with a loud voice Lord, lay not this**

sin to their charge. And when he had said this, he fell asleep. Acts 7:59-60."

"That is very close, I don't think I could be that brave," Adam admitted.

"Then Herod killed James with a sword and took Peter to prison. He had Peter well-guarded, bound with chains between two soldiers, and more at the door. But an angel of the Lord freed him. All these stories are from Acts."

"I've read Acts but I need to really study it." Adam met Nicole's eyes. "Have they told you that I've started witnessing to other men in here?"

"Adam, I'm so proud of you." Nicole felt tears forming.

"Thank you." He was humble.

"And Paul, who you remind me of, we've already talked about how he was very strong in his faith," Nicole reminded him. "Paul is not the only one but it's his story I'm most familiar with. One time Paul was in prison in Damascus and the Jews were planning to kill him, but the disciples came at night and lowered him down the wall in a basket."

"He was really persecuted then, wasn't he?" Adam was still stunned that she'd compared him to Paul.

"Yes," she stood and stretched, "but he never felt like you would expect a person undergoing that persecution would feel."

"What do you mean?" Adam asked.

"Well, from prison he wrote: **Rejoice in the Lord always, and again I say, Rejoice. Philippians 4:4."**

"He was incredible," Adam admitted.

"Yes, he was," Nicole agreed, "and I'm late. I'm sorry but I've got to go."

Chapter Nineteen

"When therefore ye shall see the abomination of desolation, spoken of by Daniel the prophet, stand in the holy place, (whoso readeth, Let him understand)."
(Matthew 24:15)

"I think we should talk about prophesies of the end times," Nicole said one day. "It's one of the things I've avoided discussing with you."

"Why? I don't mean why talk about it, I mean why have you avoided it?"

"Because I'm sorry to say, I don't know it well enough." She paused and took a deep breath. "End time prophesies are confusing. It seems as if there are as many interpretations as there are people who have read and studied the verses. For me, I try to be a good Christian and put my faith in the Lord to handle the end of times and the second coming of the Lord."

"I see," Adam said, "but I'd like to learn more."

"I would too. We'll start on it, but to study this, you should read the books of Daniel and Revelation between our visits," she pointed out. "Remember there are Biblical scholars who devote their whole lives to studying the end times. Some people think Daniel is the key to Revelation. We'll start with some verses today and talk more when you've read them. Let's start with Daniel 9."

"Okay." Adam opened his Bible.

"Daniel had visions from the angel Gabriel," she began. "Most of the controversy comes from what is called Daniel's 70 weeks prophecy. I think it's misunderstood because it means the non-believing Jews missed it, big time. It foretells the year of Christ's birth, baptism, and Crucifixion. Also, his second coming."

"In other words, they misread very important signs," Adam said.

"In Daniel 8, Daniel received a vision about 2,300 years of time but Daniel collapsed and didn't hear the entire interpretation of the vision at the time. **And I Daniel fainted, and was sick certain days; afterward I rose up and did the king's business; and I was astonished at the vision, but none understood it. Daniel 8:27.**"

"What a terrible thing to happen to him, to miss part of a very important vision. What did he do?" He was intrigued.

"He prayed. **And I prayed unto the Lord my God, and made my confession, and said, O Lord, the great and dreadful God, keeping the covenant and mercy to them that love him, and to them that keep his commandments. We have sinned and committed iniquity, and have done wickedly, and have rebelled, even by departing from thy precepts and from thy judgments. Daniel 9:4-5.** After his prayers he was shown the complete vision."

"And what was the vision?"

"It was a timetable for the end of days." Nicole sipped her soda.

"What?" Adam was astonished. "What does that mean?"

"Well, this is a long quote, he said: **Seventy weeks are determined upon thy people and thy holy city, to finish the transgression, and to make an end of sins, and to make reconciliation for iniquity, and to bring in everlasting righteousness, and to seal up the vision and prophecy, and to anoint the most holy. Know therefore and understand, that from the going forth of the commandment to restore and to build Jerusalem unto the Messiah the Prince that shall be seven weeks, and threescore and two weeks: the street shall be built again, and the wall, even in troublous times. And after threescore and two weeks shall Messiah be cut off, but not for himself: and the people of the prince that** shall come shall destroy the city and the sanctuary; and the end thereof shall be with a flood, and unto the end of the war desolations are determined. And he shall confirm the covenant with many for one week and in the midst of the week he shall cause the sacrifice and the oblation to cease, and for the overspreading of abominations he shall make it desolate, even until the consummation. And that determined shall be poured upon the desolate. Daniel 9:24-27."

"Again I say, what?" Adam rubbed his face. "I need help."

"So do I," Nicole admitted. "In Jeremiah, we're told: **And this whole land shall be a desolation, and an astonishment; and these nations shall serve the king of Babylon seventy years. And it shall come to pass, when seventy years are accomplished, that I will punish the king of Babylon, and that nation saith the Lord, for their iniquity, and the land of the Chaldeans, and will make it perpetual desolations. Jeremiah 25:11-12.**"

"Sounds very grim." Adam frowned.

"It goes on to say: **For they prophesy a lie unto you, to remove you far from your land; and that I should drive you out, and ye should perish. Jeremiah 27:10.**" She paused. "But there's hope: **For thus saith the Lord, that after seventy years shall be accomplished at Babylon I will visit you and perform my good word toward you, in causing you to return to this place. Jeremiah 29:10.**"

"It turns out that Gabriel's vision was about the time of wrath during God's anger with Israel because of its rebellion against Him. It will continue until Christ returns. It talks about God's wrath against his people, how they will fall and be taken prisoner to different nations. Jerusalem, it says, will be trampled on by the Gentiles. There was a kind of preview of the tribulation under Antiochus IV. He was not a nice guy at all, but his reign ended on God's schedule, and so will the Antichrist's," she told Adam, who still looked confused.

"The Antichrist?" His eyes seemed tired. "What or who is the Antichrist?"

"We'll talk more about him later." Her smile seemed tired. "Don't worry."

"Because the Jews disobeyed God's law Antiochus was allowed to persecute Israel. Today things are just as bad and we're all open to another madman."

"Why?" Adam asked defiantly. "Can't God control man?"

"He gave us all free will. We're his children, not his puppets," she snapped. "Man has no excuse. We've been warned. The Antichrist will be much worse than Antiochus was. He might be alive today already, but he is hidden until the time for him to appear. The Antichrist will attempt to rule the world, and the world will let him. Three and one-half years after the start of the Tribulation-"

"What is the tribulation?" Adam interjected. "I know, more on that later."

"As I was saying," she grinned, "the Antichrist will take control of what is called the revived Roman Empire and then will try to rule the world. But Christ will destroy his empire. Just like when Hitler took over Germany, and tried to take over the world. Some people, maybe many people, thought World War II was the tribulation and Hitler was the Antichrist, but far worse is yet to come."

"Not too cheerful here," Adam groaned.

"Remember though, God is in control. He wants us to be ready, at any moment."

"Ready for what?"

"That depends on who you're talking to," Nicole admitted, "the second coming or the rapture. Personally, I think we should prepare for both."

"I can understand the second coming," Adam said, "but what is the rapture?"

"The rapture is the belief that Christ will take his believers with him and then return at Armageddon to defeat the Antichrist. Christians do not have to look forward with dread because we are saved by Jesus. **For God hath not appointed us to wrath, but to obtain salvation by our Lord Jesus Christ. 1 Thessalonians 5:9.**"

"Praise God." He was relieved.

"Now here comes the tricky part. Some people do not believe in the rapture, they say the word rapture is not even in the Bible," Nicole admitted.

"But the Bible wasn't written in English!" Adam protested.

"Exactly!" Nicole smiled, pleased at his insight. "I looked it up in the dictionary for the word's origin. I always thought that Rapture came from the same root as raptor, or birds of prey that snatch up their victims, that word comes from the Latin Rapare, for birds or even dinosaurs that seize and carry off their victims. I thought, in this case, Jesus would seize and carry off his faithful."

"That sounds good," he admitted.

"But I also found the Latin word Raptus which means passion of ecstasy, or being carried away by overwhelming emotion. So to me, rapture is in the Bible, it's just lost in the translation, or should I say hidden."

"What do you mean?"

"I mean it was lost in the translation into English, waiting for the time to be right for us to find it. **For the Lord himself shall descend from heaven with a shout, with the voice of the Archangel, and with the trump of God, and the dead in Christ shall rise first. Then we which are alive and remain shall be caught up together with them in the clouds, to meet the Lord in the air: and so shall we ever be with the Lord. 1 Thessalonians 4:16-17.**"

"That does sound like the rapture you're talking about."

"Most of those who turn to God after the rapture will be

martyred. It's terrible beyond anything the world has ever known. So the time to be saved is now. We want to save anyone we can from what's coming. There are people who need to hear the gospel. Without Christ, there is no hope! If anyone says Christians are pushy, that is why."

"Pushy like you?" His face was a picture of innocence as he teased her.

She grinned. "Daniel 9 is not symbolic, it's a very important um, calendar of the time to come; a blueprint that prophesy is built on. This is set in 539 B.C. It was the first year of King Darius' reign. By the way, you should read Daniel's prayer in chapter 9, it's amazing. This prophesy is about Israel, not just the church. Israel is still sinning, it is still estranged from God. Israel doesn't get the vision or the prophesy; so their most Holy Place is covered over today by the Muslim's Dome of the Rock. All the predictions of this vision are in the future. The question is how do we know how long the seventy sevens are? In the Old Testament sevens can stand for days, years and weeks of years, and a year was 360 days. That's where the confusion comes into play, not everyone agrees about the dates. I think that most people believe Gabriel's prediction concerns the seventy weeks that begin in 444 B.C., and the exact time that the Messiah would be crucified on the cross. When the Messiah was crucified the promises of the covenant with Abraham was also cut off until His second coming."

"Why was God so angry?" Adam wondered. "I mean, he was already angered, but this seems worse."

"Well, as you pointed out, he was already angry, but after Christ's death most Jews lied about Him and persecuted His disciples. That made his anger worse, I think. So then there was a period of great destruction for the Jews. They were slaughtered, sold into slavery and scattered around the world in A.D. 70. Not only had the nation killed Jesus Christ, but God killed off the nation of Israel and they would not become a sovereign nation again until May 14, 1948."

"Do the dates match the timeline?"

"Yes. Additionally, the prophecy of the seventy sevens reveals what it will be like during the times of the tribulations. There will be wars, natural disasters such as volcanoes and earthquakes, and plagues until His second coming," she told him. "Jesus predicts that the Jews will be deceived by the Antichrist. **I have come in my Father's name, and you do not accept me; but if someone else comes in his own name, you will accept him. John 5:43.**"

"I understand now why He is so angry." Adam's voice was quiet but firm.

"The Tribulation is the seventieth seven of Gabriel's prophecy. Revelation chapters 6-19 which we'll cover next time, describes it in detail. The tribulation is divided into two halves, the second half is known as the Great Tribulation. The Antichrist will stop all worship at Israel's Temple and exalt himself over God and force the world to worship him and his image. The abomination that causes desolation will end. This is the time that the Antichrist will put an end to sacrifices and offerings until the end that is decreed is poured out on him. This happens when Christ returns in all His glory and defeats him at Armageddon."

"Will He come soon?"

"I believe He will come any day now," she smiled, "any day."

"So what's next?" Adam wondered.

"Next we study Revelation." Her smile was wicked. "Read it tonight, and Adam..."

"What?"

"Read it carefully. Daniel was pretty straightforward." She grinned. "Revelation is um, very complicated."

As she left the room, Adam was banging his head on the table. She laughed.

When she got to her car, she banged her head on the steering wheel.

Chapter Twenty

"Blessed is he that readeth, and they that hear the words of this prophecy, and keep those things which are written therein: for the time is at hand."
(Revelation 1:3)

"Well, did you take my suggestion and read Revelation?" Nicole smiled at Adam.

"Yes, I did," Adam told her, "even though I got confused while I was reading it."

"So you did find it difficult to understand? And confusing?"

"Yes, it was confusing."

"I thought so too, which is funny because like the book's title means, everything is revealed." Nicole smiled softly. "I'm no expert so if we cover this, it's from a normal person's point of view. I will probably mess some things up."

"Okay, I understand."

"I've been wanting to go into it in some detail, are you game?"

At his nod, she began, "Well it starts as John sends greetings to the seven churches, he sends them grace and peace and speaks of Christ's return: **Behold, he cometh with clouds; and every eye shall see him, and they also which pierced him: and all kindreds of the earth shall wail because of him. Even so, Amen. Revelation 1:7.** Did you notice that it says the ones who pierced him, meaning crucified him, shall see him?"

"Yes, and it talks about kindreds of the earth wailing because of him. Are those the ones who had rejected him?" Adam asked.

"I think so, yes."

He leaned back in the chair. "I wouldn't want to be one of them. I was, but not anymore, thanks to you."

"You are very welcome." She smiled and continued reading. **"I am the Alpha and the Omega, the first and the last, and what thou seest write in a book and send it unto the seven churches which are in Asia, unto Ephesus and unto Smyrna, and unto Pergamos, and unto Thyatira, and unto Sardis and unto Philadelphia, and unto Laodicea. Revelation 1:11.** So Christ wanted John to write his visions down and send them to these seven churches."

"That makes sense, and then it says that he turned to see the voice who spoke to him and saw the Son of Man standing in the midst of seven golden candlesticks. To me, that means the seven candlesticks are the seven churches. So Christ is the center of the churches." Adam smiled. "Am I right?"

"I believe so, keep going."

"So he writes to the church at Ephesus, and he complains about those who need to remember how they loved the church at first, but have forgotten their first love and devotion. He wants them to repent and go back to their first works."

"That happens, people come to Christ but slowly the earthly world creeps in and they move away from the church," Nicole told him.

Adam read the verses, and put them into his own words. "Next he writes to the church at Smyrna. He told them that even though they are going through tribulation, they were rich. Shouldn't they have lost their possessions during a tribulation? If they held true to their Christian faith, he would give them the crown of life, and they would not suffer the second death."

"Next, he writes to the church of Pergamos," Adam continued. "And he writes about some of the people there who believe in Balaam, who was a prophet who had turned against God and taught Balak how to seduce the men of Israel into fornicating and holding an idolatrous feast. They also had people who followed Nicolaitanes who believed the laws do not matter because God's grace covers them. Then he ordered them to repent."

Nicole took the next church. "The citizens of Thyatira were mostly poor and humble laborers. Their sin was that they let Jezebel teach. A woman represents a church in prophesy. Obviously a pure woman is a pure Church and an impure woman represents an impure Church. Jezebel was a very impure woman who never repented. He told the church to repent. And the church at Sardis was told not to be dead while still alive, they needed to wake up and be watchful, so Christ could give them more light."

"They were asleep on the job, so to speak," Adam commented.

"And he warned them: **Remember therefore how thou hast received and heard, and hold fast, and repent. If therefore thou shalt not watch, I will come on thee as a thief, and thou shalt not know what hour I will come upon thee. Revelation 3:3.** A good warning for us all," Nicole finished.

"And in Philadelphia he writes: **I know thy works: behold, I have set before thee an open door, and no man can shut it: for thou hast a little strength, and hast kept my word, and hast not denied my name. Revelation 3:8.** He tells them because they've kept the word, he will keep them from the temptation which will come to the world. He tells them to hold fast, and that if they do, they will become a pillar in the temple of God." Adam sipped his water. "We sure have temptation today."

"All around us," Nicole agreed.

"The Church of Laodicea he calls neither hot nor cold but lukewarm. I think that describes far too many Christians in the world now. In fact, he would prefer us either hot or cold, he said he would spit us out for being lukewarm. He also says: **Because thou sayest, I am rich, and increased with goods, and have need of nothing; and knowest not that thou are wretched, and miserable, and poor, and blind, and naked. Revelation 3:17.** They don't know how poor they are spiritually," Adam read and commented.

"Two of the most beautiful verses in the Bible come next: **As many as I love, I rebuke and chasten: be zealous therefore, and repent. Behold, I stand at the door, and knock: if any man hear my voice, and open the door, I will come in to him, and will sup with him, and he with me. Revelation 3:19-20.** That covers the letters to the churches, now we get into the hard part."

She gritted her teeth and read on. "This is not a continuation of the letters to the churches. John is now introducing a new vision. He sees a door opened in heaven and he saw a throne and heard a voice like a trumpet inviting him to enter. He is going to be shown things that will happen in the future. He saw Christ sitting on the throne, covered with jasper, and sardine stones, and a rainbow. There were twenty-four elders sitting around the throne, and seven lamps of fire burning before the throne. The lamps are the seven spirits of God. In front of the throne was a sea of glass and around the throne were four beasts full of eyes. The first beast was like a lion, the second like a calf, the third had a man's face, and the fourth was like an eagle. Day and night they praised God saying Holy, Holy Holy, Lord God almighty. To understand the four beasts, you need to remember that when Israel was in the wilderness the tribes were divided into four groups with the symbols of the lion, the man, the ox, and the eagle. The symbols also represent Christ, the lion means his kingship, the man is his humanity, the ox his service and sacrifice, his divinity. The eagle's eyes suggest vigilance." Nicole paused and got up to get more water.

She continued, "The elders fall down before him, toss their crowns before the throne and say: You are worthy, O Lord, to receive glory and honor and power: for you have created all things, and for your pleasure they are and were created."

Nicole looked up, "Oh, we're up to the seals. John says that he saw one sitting on the throne that had a book in his right hand that was sealed with seven seals. An angel asked in a loud voice: Who is worthy to unseal the book and open it? No man was worthy but the lion of the tribe of Judah can open the book and break the seven seals. In the middle of everything, the throne, the elders, and the four beasts there stood a lamb that had been killed, he had seven horns and seven eyes. A horn is a symbol of power, and the seven eyes are the seven spirits of God. He took the book out of the hand of him that was sitting on the throne. And the beasts and elders fell down before the lamb, singing praise that he was worthy to open the seals because he was killed and redeemed us to God with his blood. There were multitudes of angels, beasts and elders singing around the throne. And every creature which is in heaven, on earth, under the earth and in the sea worshiped and praised him." She looked up at Adam. "Your turn."

"Jesus opened one of the seals and one of the four beasts said: Come and see, and I saw a white horse, and the rider had a bow and a crown, and went out conquering. The white horse is a symbol of purity, the bow symbolizes God's word. The crown symbolizes a wreath of victory, so conquering means winning people to Jesus," Adam said, hesitating as he thought. "And when the second seal was opened a red horse came out. Red is the color of two things, sin and blood. So the rider of the red horse has the power to take peace from the earth and cause war."

"Wow! Very good Adam!" Nicole was really surprised.

"The third was a black horse, the exact opposite of the white horse. The rider holds scales, the kind that balances two sides. The scales represent judgment, but the oil and the wine were not supposed to be hurt, they were meant to be preserved. The voice says not to hurt the oil and wine. The oil means light. I think it means the light of the Holy Spirit living inside us. I'm not sure about the wine but I think it might represent doctrine. We are supposed to preserve doctrine." He paused. "The pale horse is next, and this one is especially dramatic: **And I looked, and** behold a pale horse: and his name that sat on him was Death, and Hell followed with him. And power was given unto them over the fourth part of the earth, to kill with sword, and with hunger, and with death, and with the beasts of the earth. Revelation 8. The faithful were persecuted in many ways, including being fed to lions."

"And when the next seal is opened, he saw the souls of those who were killed for the word of God and their testimony under the altar. They were calling out for God to avenge them and punish the ones who persecuted them. Why are they under the altar if they died for God's word?" Nicole wondered. "I think this has to do with the layout of the temple. I don't think it means they were being um, slighted. I think it means their blood was poured out at the base of the altar on the earth. They are given white robes, a symbol of righteousness, and told to wait a while." She answered her own question.

"When the sixth seal was opened, wow, there was a great earthquake, and the sun went black, probably from the ash, and the moon looked blood red. There were showers of falling stars, like the fruit falling off a tree shaken by a very strong wind. And the heavens opened up, moving mountains and islands. This is a very massive earthquake. It happens when Christ returns, this is the second coming." Adam's eyes were wide. "And the kings, the rich, and the mighty, well, everyone who is not saved will hide, some in caves, and they will even ask the mountains to hide them from Christ's anger. They never prayed to Him, but now they pray to be hidden **from** Him. It's too late, they cannot conceal their guilt or escape their punishment."

"I'll take chapter 7, and we can trade off, okay," Nicole asked. Adam nodded and she began. "After the sixth seal, four angels, the faithful, are holding the four corners of the earth; in other words the whole earth. They are holding back the winds of destruction. Another angel comes from the east with the seal of the living God. He cries out to the four angels and tells them not to hurt the earth until the servants of the living God are sealed. There were 144,000 of the tribes of Israel; 12,000 from each of the twelve tribes. After this, a multitude so great no man could count them stood before the throne of God and Jesus, clothed in white robes and saying salvation to our God and to the Lamb. Around them were the angels, the elders, and the four beasts. They fell and worshiped God, saying Amen, Blessing, Glory, Wisdom, glory and thanksgiving honor, power, and might unto God forever, amen." She paused.

"One of the elders asked who the people in the multitude were and he said, you know, they are the ones who came out of the great tribulation, and have washed the blood from their robes, making them white and pure in the blood of the lamb." She began again, "Because of the experience of going through the tribulation and their victory over sin because of Christ, they are very near to God and desire to serve Him. In heaven they will never face hunger or thirst again. They will not be burned or blinded by the sun, Christ will free them and lead them to the living water, and God shall wipe the tears from their eyes."

Adam started his chapter, which was chapter 8. "When the seventh seal is opened there was silence in heaven, why?" He answered himself. "Before this there was continual praise in heaven. I think the silence is because there is no one there, except God. I think the angels, and everyone else is with Christ. This is the second coming. I'm not sure about the time, but it must be time measured by God's time, not measured by a clock on the wall."

"I agree, and I think it's easy to get bogged down with time instead of the message." Nicole sighed.

"The seven angels are each given a trumpet. Trumpets are associated with warning or signaling a war. Another angel stands in front of the altar, and he offered a lot of incense, with the prayers of the saints to the golden altar before the throne. The throne of God?" He wondered.

"I think so." She nodded

"And the angel is Christ?"

"Again, I think so."

"The smoke from the incense rose to God. The angel took the censer and filled it with fire and cast it to the earth, which means the incense was gone and the intercession is over, and there were voices and thunder, lightning and an earthquake."

"You've really studied the books and online studies I sent you." Nicole was proud of him.

"The first trumpet sounded, followed by hail and fire mingled with blood, which burned trees and green grass. The second trumpet sounded and a great mountain, or nation, burning, was cast into the sea. And a third of the sea turned to blood, and a third of the sea creatures died, and a third of the ships were destroyed. Then the third trumpet sounded and a great star fell from heaven, a star is the symbol of a leader, and a falling star is an apostate leader. Was this a meteorite? It fell on the third part of the rivers. The name of the star is wormwood which means bitterness, so wherever this leader went he caused bitterness, and many men died because of it."

He sipped some water. "The fourth trumpet sounded and a third of the sun, moon, and stars were damaged. Does that mean darkened? These were the leaders, their consuls, and the senate. So these are extinguished."

"Who'd miss them?" Nicole said dryly.

"And there was an angel saying woe, woe, woe to the unrighteous because of the other trumpets yet to come."

Nicole took up her chapter. "The fifth trumpet sounded and a star fell from heaven, remember a fallen star is an apostate leader. To this fallen leader is given a key to the bottomless pit. Smoke rose out of the pit as he opened it, so much smoke that the sun and air were dark. The sun is Jesus and his word. So the smoke from the bottomless pit is the opposite of the light and hides the truth, and locusts came out of the smoke. They came from the false teachings and were given power by the lies from the false prophets, but they were ordered not to hurt the earth or any green thing or trees. They could only hurt those without the seal of God. And to them, they were told not to kill them but to torment them five months. I think the order not to kill them applies to the whole group and not to the individual people. The time period? Again, I'm not thinking it's our time, but is based on God's time. The torment causes tremendous pain but not death, like a scorpion sting. It's so bad that men seek death, but don't find it." She shrugged her shoulders. "The shape of the locusts were like horses prepared for battle, I'm not sure of what that means, but the golden crowns on their heads? A turban, richly embroidered. They had men's faces, with beards, and long hair. The teeth? Symbolic of how they tore into their victims. They wore breastplates of iron, and made a loud sound. I've heard some people think the locusts are helicopters, and that John was describing something he had no other words for. It's possible. They had tails like scorpions with the power to hurt men. Their ruler was the angel of the bottomless pit. His name means destroyer. I looked it up. This is the first woe, two more to come."

"Not very encouraging, is it?" Adam got more water.

Nicole ignored his comment and continued, "The sixth trumpet sounded and a voice from the altar before God told the sixth angel to loosen the four angels that are held in the river Euphrates. And the angels were let loose to kill a third of the men. The army was huge, two hundred thousand thousand. I don't think such a large army was possible until today; no country had enough men. China does now, for whatever it's worth. The ones riding had breastplates, and the heads of the horses were as the heads of lions, does that represent strength and ferocity? And out of their mouths came fire, smoke, and brimstone which killed a third of the men. The serpent tail I think refers to lies. The ones that were not killed by these plagues and did not repent still worshiped devils and idols and refused to repent of their murders, fornication, and thefts."

"There seems to be a gap at the start of chapter 10," Adam said. "The next trumpet does not sound yet. John has other things to tell us, and he does it here. He says he saw another angel descend from heaven, this one is clothed in clouds, and has a rainbow on his head. The rainbow represents God's covenant. His face, as if it were the sun, is like Christ. The feet, I think, means his legs, not just his feet. This is Jesus. And he had a little book in his hand. Daniel? It's open. One foot on the earth and one on the sea, covering the whole world. The message in this book is worldwide. He makes a loud shout like that of a lion roaring, and seven thunders uttered something but before John could write down what was said he heard a voice from heaven telling him not to write them down."

Adam paused, just resting for a moment. "And Jesus lifted his hand to heaven and swears on Himself, that there should no longer be time. Are the days of the seventh angel, a reference to the seventh trumpet? I'm not sure but the seventh trumpet sounds and the mystery of God will be finished. I'm not sure what the mystery is."

"If you were, it wouldn't be a mystery, would it?" Nicole grinned.

"The voice from heaven told John to go take the open book which is in the hand of the angel. So John went to the angel and told him to give him the book. The angel told him to eat it up, or get so much into it that it fills him. It will make your belly bitter, but it will be sweet as honey in your mouth. So John did, and it was sweet and made his belly bitter. And he was told to prophesy again, before many people, nations, tongues and kings." Adam finished.

"Adam, I need to get home." Nicole stood up and stretched a bit. "We'll keep going next time. This is easier than I thought, going chapter by chapter and verse by verse. We may make a mistake but we're trying."

Chapter Twenty-one

"I Jesus have sent mine angel to testify unto you these things in the churches. I am the root and the offspring of David, and the bright and morning star."
(Revelation 22:16)

"Where did we leave off last time?" Nicole asked.

"John had just been told to eat the sweet and bitter book at the end of chapter 10."

"So I've got chapter 11." Nicole opened her Bible and looked at her notes. "John was given a reed to use for measuring, and was told to rise and measure the temple and the worshipers. Measure their character? But don't measure the court of the gentiles and Jerusalem will be crushed underfoot for a time. There will be two witnesses who will speak their prophesies for a time. They will be dressed in sackcloth, which indicates mourning or distress. These witnesses are also referred to as the two olive trees and the two candlesticks. If any man tries to hurt them fire will come out of their mouth and kill them. These have the power to shut heaven so that it won't rain in the days of their prophesy, and have the power to turn water to blood, and to send plagues when they finish their testimony, the beast will wage war against them and kill them, and their bodies will lay in the street, probably in Jerusalem. People around the world will see their dead bodies for a time, and prevent them from being buried, in fact they'll rejoice over them because their prophesies hit their conscience. Then the two witnesses will rise up from the dead and scare those who see them."

"That would scare me!" Adam interjected.

"Me too, if I hadn't read this." She continued, "Then the witnesses heard a voice from heaven call them and they went up to heaven on a cloud while their enemies watched. The same hour there was a great earthquake, and a tenth of the city fell, killing seven thousand men and scaring the rest, who gave glory to God. Now the second woe is past, and the third woe comes quickly. The seventh angel sounded, and voices in Heaven sang: The kingdoms of this world are become [the kingdoms] of our Lord, and of his Christ; and he shall reign for ever and ever." She paused, smiling. "Have you ever heard Handel's Messiah?"

"No."

"Part of it is called the Hallelujah chorus, I'll bring it and play it for you. He uses these words as lyrics. It's fantastic. Anyway the four and twenty elders fell on their faces to worship God."

"The nations band together, angry, because they don't want to face judgment and resent the rewards given to those who serve God. God's heavenly temple was opened with the ark of his testament. There was thundering, and lightning, and an earthquake and hail. It was the seventh plague," she finished. "Your turn."

Adam started chapter 12.

"There appeared a woman clothed with the sun, with the moon under her feet, and a crown of twelve stars on her head; she was pregnant and in labor. The church is portrayed as beautiful, delicate, and pure, a virgin. Then a red dragon appeared in heaven. The dragon had seven heads and ten horns, with seven crowns on his head. His tail cast down a third of the stars, leaders in heaven, to earth. He stood before the woman who was in labor ready to devour her child as soon as it was born. She gave birth to Jesus who was to rule all the nations. He was taken up to God and his throne, and she fled to the wilderness where she had a place to stay and be cared for that was prepared for her by God. There was war in heaven, Michael, Christ, and his angels fought against the red dragon, Satan, and his angels. Satan and his angels lost the war and were cast out of heaven."

"Of course," Nicole interjected. "Don't they get it yet? Christ wins and Satan and his followers end up paying the price for their defiance."

"Evidently they don't but they will." Adam continued, "There was joy because Satan was cast out, letting the salvation and strength and kingdom of God emerge, and Satan the accuser is cast down. Christ and his angels won over Satan by the blood of the lamb, their testimony, and because they would die before betraying God. So if you're in heaven, rejoice, and if you're on earth or the sea, woe, for the devil is bound to the earth. And the church is still being persecuted. The devil is infuriated because he knows he only has a short time left. So the devil persecuted the woman who had borne the child, Jesus, and the woman is the church. And the woman was given wings like an eagle so she could fly to that place in the wilderness, where she could stay and be nourished. Water came out of Satan's mouth to try to flood the woman out but the earth helped the woman by swallowing the flood waters. The dragon was furious with the woman and tried to destroy the Christian church which kept the commandments of God and witnessed for Christ.

"Poor loser," Nicole commented.

"Yeah," Adam sneered. "He is. But whoever said the dragon was a nice guy?"

Adam took a deep breath. "In chapter 13 John saw the beast rise out of the sea with seven heads, with crowns and ten horns. The crowns show that the seven heads are heads of state or in power. Upon his heads were names of blasphemy, meaning a false prophet? The beast was made of several animals and got his power from Satan. The beast had a head wound, he was wounded almost to death but he recovered. The world was amazed and began to worship him, saying who can stand up to him? And he spoke blasphemies against God, his church and all who were in heaven. Everyone on earth whose name was not written in the book of life worshiped him. They were led into captivity, and those who killed by the sword, were themselves killed with the sword. This is where the saints really need patience and faith."

"And John saw another beast with two horns like a lamb, who spoke like a dragon, persecuting the church and he caused people to worship the first beast, the one who had almost died, but lived. He did great wonders and deceived men so much that they made an image of the beast. The beast had power to give life to that image so that the image would speak. It caused any who would not worship the beast to be killed and everyone receive a mark on their hand or forehead, so that no one could buy or sell without the mark, the number of the beast is 666."

"The lamb stood on Mt. Zion with the hundred and forty-four thousand, and His Father's name on their forehead," Nicole began. "And a voice from heaven sang a new song before the throne, and the four beasts, and the elders. No one could learn the song except for the 144,000 which were saved. These are not stained by the false churches, they are innocent. They follow the lamb and are the ones offered to God and the Lamb. The Israelites offered their first fruits as their offering. They had no guile or deception. And an angel came with the message, for the whole world to revere God, and give him glory because the hour of judgment has come. The next angel said Babylon is fallen because she made all nations accept false doctrines and taste the wrath of God, through an evil connection between the church and state. Instead the church should be connected to God. And the last angel said that if any man worships the beast and his image or have his mark they will feel God's wrath, which is poured out into his indignation, and they shall be tormented with fire and brimstone in the presence of his holy angels and Jesus, forever and ever. Those who worship the beast have no rest. The patience and faithfulness of the saints, who keep the commandments of God and Jesus are blessed, and the dead which die in the Lord, who may rest from their labor and their good works follow them."

"John saw Christ on a white cloud, wearing a golden crown

and holding a sickle to reap the harvest. An angel came out of the temple and said to Christ, use your sickle and reap, because the time has come for the harvest. And Jesus thrust his sickle into the ground and the earth was reaped, meaning the righteous were gathered. Another angel told Christ to use his sickle to gather the vines of the earth for the grapes are ripe. And Christ used his sickle to gather the vines and tossed them into the winepress of God's anger. And the wine was crushed outside the city, completely destroying the evil hosts," she finished.

"In chapter 15," Adam started, "there was another great sign in heaven, seven angels with the seven last plagues. They are the end of the wrath of God, the punishment of the worshipers of the beast; those who had received the warning and rejected the beast had been saved by Christ's blood and were now secure in the kingdom of God. They even stood loyal when the beast ordered their deaths, and they sang praises to the Lamb, Lord God Almighty, saying great and marvelous are your works, just and true are your ways, who does not revere you and glorify your name? The temple of the tabernacle in heaven was opened and seven angels came out, and one of the four beasts gave the seven angels seven golden vials filled with the wrath of God. The temple filled with smoke from the glory of God, and no man could enter the temple until the seven plagues from the seven angels were done."

"And the voice from heaven, was it God?"

"I think so," Adam answered Nicole's rhetorical question.

"It told the seven angels to pour out the vial of the wrath of God on the earth. And the first angel poured out his vial which caused painful and severe sores on the men with the mark of the beast, and those who worshiped his image. The second angel poured out his vial into the sea, killing every living thing. And the third angel caused the rivers and fountains to become blood. And the angel of the waters said, you are just for they have shed the blood of the saints, now you give them blood to drink. Another angel said Lord God, your judgments are true and righteous. The fourth angel poured his vial on the sun and scorched men with fire. The men who were scorched blasphemed and did not repent. The fifth angel poured his vial on the throne of the beast and his kingdom turned dark, so dark and cold that they bit their tongues in pain and they blasphemed God because of their pain and did not repent. The sixth angel dried up the Euphrates and unclean spirits came out of the dragon, the beast and the false prophet, and these devils went to gather them for the battle with God. He gathered them together in a place called Armageddon."

"Behold, I come as a thief. Blessed is he that watcheth, and keepeth his garments, lest he walk naked, and they see his shame. Revelation 16:15. The seventh angel poured his vial in the air and the voice of God came from his temple saying, it is done. And there were voices, and thunder and lightning, and the worst earthquake ever. And Babylon was divided into three parts, the cities of the nations fell, as God gave Babylon the wine of his wrath. And islands and mountains disappeared. There was a hailstorm with massive hailstones, and men blasphemed God because of the hail. It says the hailstones were about the weight of a talent, I looked it up and it was estimated at over fifty pounds."

"That could kill a man." Adam looked up as though there could be hailstones coming down inside the small visiting room. "Let's see what happens next, in chapter 17."

"One of the seven angels with vials said come here, I will show you the sentence of the great whore that has power over many nations," Adam started. "Who the kings of the earth have fornicated with and who have been made drunk on Satan's deceptions. So he took me, in spirit, to the wilderness and I saw a woman, apostate people, on a scarlet beast, full of blasphemy with seven heads and ten horns. She was covered with purple and scarlet, and gold and precious stones. She had a cup in her hand full of abominations and the filth of her fornication. On her forehead it said, Mystery, Babylon the great, the mother of harlots and abominations of the earth. She was drunk with the blood of the saints and martyrs of Jesus. When I saw her, I was amazed. The angel asked why I was amazed, and said I will tell you about the woman and the beast that carried her with seven heads and ten horns. This beast had been active but disappeared. It will come from the bottomless pit and go to destruction, and the people who were not written in the book of life will wonder when they behold the beast. And the seven heads, heads of state, are seven mountains, or places, the woman sits on. There are seven kings, five are gone, defeated, one still exists and one is yet to come, and must remain a short time. The beast that was and is no longer is an eighth, who comes out of the seven, and goes to perdition." Adam paused. "The ten horns are ten kings, who get their power from the beast only, they are not heads of state. They have one thing in mind, to give the capability and authority to the beast. They go on to make war on Christ, and lose. And he was told the waters where the whore sat are peoples, nations and tongues. And the ten horns shall hate the whore, they will make her desolate and naked, they will eat her flesh and burn her up. For God has put it in their hearts and minds to carry out his will against her. And to give their kingdom to the beast until God's word is complete. And the woman is the city that rules over the kings of the earth."

Nicole moved on to chapter 18.

"After this, he saw another angel come down from heaven with great power and glory. That angel said Babylon is fallen and has become the home of devils and foul spirits, and a cage of every unclean bird. All nations have swallowed her fornication, and the kings of the earth have committed fornication with her, and merchants have become rich from her. And a voice from heaven said, come out of her, do not participate in her sins so you do not get her punishments. Her sins have reached heaven and God remembers those sins. Her cup of punishment is doubly filled. Whatever amount she has glorified herself with and lived in sin that much sorrow give her, because in her mind she's a queen; she acts as if she's Christ's bride, but she is not. She does not expect anything bad to happen to her, she thinks she can get away with her deception. She's very wrong. So her plagues will come, death and mourning and famine. She will be burned up because the Lord God who judged her, is strong. And the kings who have fornicated with her and lived evilly with her shall mourn her when they see the smoke from her burning. They stand far off to avoid her torment, and say: Wow, great city of Babylon, in an instant your punishment has come. The merchants weep and mourn because no one will buy their corrupt merchandise anymore. They want nothing to do with anything from Babylon, not gold, silver, precious stones, or anything, even slaves or the souls of men. The fruits you desired are gone, your luxury is gone, and you will never find them again. The merchants who were made rich by her stood off in the distance, afraid, and weeping and wailing, saying that this great city was so rich! And now it's gone. And the ship captains and sailors stood far off and cried, asking what city is like this city? And they threw dust on their heads and wailed, because the city made all the mariners rich, and now they are desolate." She paused for some water. "Rejoice over her, heaven and holy apostles and prophets, for God has avenged you. A strong angel took a large millstone and threw it into the sea, saying, that with sudden violence Babylon is torn down, and gone forever. The musicians will not be heard again, and the craftsmen will be gone, all manufacturing has ceased. There will be no more light, all social life will end. Your merchants were great men of the earth, and your deceptions deceived all nations. In her was the blood of prophets and saints, and of all that were slain on earth."

"Next, John heard a voice from crowds in heaven saying Alleluia and power to the Lord our God. For his judgments are true and righteous. He judged the great whore who corrupted the earth and avenged the blood of his servants. And the four beasts and the twenty four elders also fell down and worshiped God. And a voice from the throne said Praise our God, you servants and followers. And the voice of great multitudes were saying Alleluia for the Lord God. Let us rejoice for the marriage of the Lamb is now, and his wife is ready. She is dressed in fine linen, clean and white. The fine linen is the righteousness of saints. And he said write, Blessed are the ones called to the marriage supper of the lamb, these are the true sayings of God. And John fell at the angel's feet to worship him and was told not to, because the angel is a fellow servant to him and to other Christians, worship God. And John saw the heavens opened and a white horse appeared, and he that sat on him was called Faithful and True, in righteousness he judges and makes war. His eyes were like fire, and on his head were many crowns; and he had a name that no man knew except himself. And he was clothed in a vestment dipped in his own blood, and his name is the Word of God."

Adam went through chapter 19. "And the armies in heaven followed Him on white horses, clothed in clean white, fine linen. And a sharp sword came out of His mouth, to smite the nations, and He shall rule them with a rod of iron and crush the evil with the fury of Almighty God. He has on his clothes KING OF KING AND LORD OF LORDS written on the thigh. John saw an angel standing in the sun, calling the birds to gather for the supper of God. So that they could eat the flesh of kings, and captives, of men and horses, and the flesh of all men, free and bond, great and small. And John saw a beast with the kings of the earth, and their armies gathered together to make war against him and his army."

"Fools," Nicole interjected. "Damned fools."

"Exactly. The beast was taken, along with the false prophet, and the two of them were cast alive into a lake of fire and brimstone, and the rest were killed with the sword that came out of the mouth of him that sat on the horse, and the birds were filled with their flesh."

"John saw an angel come down from heaven, with the key to the bottomless pit and a huge chain in his hand," Nicole said as she started chapter twenty. "He laid ahold of the dragon, Satan, and bound him for a thousand years and cast him into the bottomless pit, and shut him up and set a seal upon him, so that he could not deceive anyone anymore, for the next thousand years. After that he must be set loose for a while. And I saw thrones, and they sat upon them had the power of judgment given unto them, and I saw the souls of them that were beheaded for the witness of Jesus, and for the word of God, and which had not worshiped the beast, or received the mark on their foreheads or their hands; and they lived and reigned with Christ a thousand years. Blessed and holy are the ones that are part of the first resurrection: the second death has no power over them, but they shall be priests of God and of Christ, and shall reign with him a thousand years. And when the thousand years are over, Satan shall be freed from his prison. He shall go out to deceive the nations which are in the four quarters of the earth, all of the unsaved. He will gather them together to battle, the number of them is so many they are as there are grains of sand in the sea, uncountable. And they went up on earth, and circled the camp of the saints and the beloved city, Jerusalem. Fire came down from God and devoured them. And the devil that deceived them was cast into the lake of fire and brimstone, where the beast and the false prophet are, and they all shall be tormented day and night for ever and ever. And I saw a great white throne and him that sat on it from whose face the earth and the heaven fled away; and there was found no place for them. And I saw the dead who were raised stand before God. The books were opened: and another book was opened, which is the book of life: and the dead were judged out of those things which were written in the books, according to their works."

She paused. "And the sea gave up the dead, and Hell delivered up the dead who were there and every man was judged by his works. And death and hell were cast into the lake of fire. And if anyone was not found written in the book of life they were cast into the lake of fire."

Adam continued, "And I saw a new heaven and earth: for the first heaven and earth were gone and there was no more sea. John saw the holy city, New Jerusalem, descending from heaven, prepared as a bride adorned for her husband, Jesus. And I heard a voice from heaven saying: Behold, the tabernacle of God is with men, and he will dwell with them, and they shall be his people and be their God." Adam said, "What a vision that must be. And God shall wipe the tears from their eyes; and there shall be no more death or sorrow, or crying, or pain: for these are gone. And he that sat upon the throne, was it Jesus?"

"I think so," Nicole replied.

"He said: See, I make all things new and He told John to write it, for this is true. And he told John, It is done. I am Alpha and Omega, the beginning and the end. I will freely give to him that thirsts water from the fountain of the water of life. He that conquers his sinful nature will inherit all things; and I will be his God, and he shall be my son. But the cowards and unbelievers, the evil ones will wind up in the lake of fire and brimstone. This is the second death."

"And one of the seven angels, which had the seven vials full of the seven last plagues, came to John and said: Come hither, I will show you the bride, the Lamb's wife. And he carried John, in spirit, to a high mountain and showed him the holy Jerusalem, descending out of heaven from God having the glory of God. Her light was like a precious stone. There was a great wall with twelve gates with an angel at each of the gates and the names written on the gates were the names of the twelve tribes of Israel. And the wall of the city had twelve foundations, named for the twelve apostles. And the angel with John had a golden reed to measure the city, the gates, and the wall. And the building in the wall was jasper: and the city was pure gold, like clear glass. And the foundations of the walls were adorned with precious stones. And the twelve gates were twelve pearls; and the street of the city was pure gold, as it were transparent glass. And I saw no temple, for the Lord God Almighty and the Lamb are the temple. And the city didn't need the sun or moon for the glory of God lit it, and the Lamb is the light. And those nations which are saved shall walk in the light of it. And the kings of the earth bring glory and honor into it. And the gates will be shut by day and there will not be night there. They shall bring glory and honor into it, and nothing that can defile or work an abomination will enter, only those which are written in the Lamb's book of life."

Adam started, "In Revelation 22, John is shown a pure river of the water of life flowing from the throne of God and the Lamb. The river, to me, sounds like salvation coming from the throne of God and the Lamb. And the tree of life, is that eternal life?"

"I think so," Nicole replied. "And I think the fruits are abundance, or all we need."

"And there will be no more curses but God and Jesus will rule and the servants, or followers of Jesus will worship him," Adam continued. "And they will be close enough to God to see his face, and the seal marks them as belonging to God."

"The light of God's presence is all the light they need. And this freedom and abundance will continue forever," Nicole added. **"And, behold, I come quickly: blessed is he that keepeth the sayings of the prophecy of this book. Revelation 22:7,** is about the second coming."

"Agreed. So when John saw and heard all of this, he fell down to worship at the feet of the angel who told him: don't worship me, we are fellow servants of God and the brethren, worship God. Don't keep these prophesies hidden or sealed away, because the time is coming soon. It sounds fairly clear to me," Adam said. He then read, **"And, behold, I come quickly; and** my reward is with me, to give every man according as his work shall be. I am Alpha and Omega, the beginning and the end, the first and the last. Blessed are they that do his commandments, that they may have right to the tree of life, and may enter in through the gates into the city. Revelation 22:12-14."

"The holy spirit and the bride, the bride is the church, say come; let whoever hears come to take the water of life freely," Nicole continued the chapter. "And then comes the warning: For I testify unto every man that heareth the words of the prophecy of this book, If any man shall add unto these things, God shall add unto him the plagues that are written in this book: And if any man shall take away from the words of the book of this prophecy, God shall take away his part out of the book of life, and out of the holy city, and from the things which are written in this book. Revelation 22:18-19. Then Jesus tells us he's coming quickly. And it ends with: The grace of our Lord Jesus Christ be with you all. Amen. Revelation 22:21."

Chapter Twenty-two

"To everything there is a season, and a time to every purpose under heaven."
(Ecclesiastes 3:1)

For years the prison visits continued and Adam grew in his walk with the Lord. He not only joined the prayer group but frequently led the discussions. He was still under attack by other Muslims who accused him of apostasy which was punishable, to the extremist Muslims in the prison, by death. He was attacked several times, but he was never injured as severely as that first attack. The guards grew to know him and watched out for him as much as they could. Nicole finally admitted to herself that she and Adam were true friends. She still went to visit him at least once a week.

Nicole also visited the families of her friends who were killed. She wanted them to know that by visiting Adam she was not forgetting their loved ones. Since they were all Christian families, they believed in forgiveness. It had been a real struggle for most of them, but they had come to peace with the tragedy. All of them had visited Adam in prison, but Hans' family had visited Adam several times. In fact, Hans' mother supported a lawyer who tried to get his sentence changed from life without parole to one with a possibility of parole. Still, even if the lawyer was successful, Adam would serve over fifty years.

Nicole's new business, the gym, continued to thrive. In fact, she now owned three gyms in three different towns, each with a children's center next door. The children's center held classes in dance aerobics, karate, and had basketball teams. All of the gyms followed her strict guidelines. There were no judgments, no focusing on weight loss or appearance, but instead placed an emphasis on self-esteem, confidence, and fitness. She had a full staff of trainers, counselors, and doctors on call at each location. There were dance aerobic classes, swimming, karate, and one location even had belly dancing classes.

Her marriage was strong, and filled with joy and passion. She had another baby, a boy named Jacob Troy, bringing the grand total to four children, the twins fathered by Adam, and two more since she married Troy. Her brother David had three. Her mother got remarried, of course, to Sid, the man Kate and Laura introduced her to, and they were very happy.

The only sad note was that Emily's mother, Mae, passed away. Although she had been afflicted with senile dementia for years, she had also been a strong Christian. They held a simple graveside ceremony and laid her to rest next to her husband Pete. Emily mourned, of course, but she seemed to find peace in her pain. Nicole put a large part of her funds into building a women's shelter. To her surprise, she was nominated by a local group for their Humanitarian of the Year award.

As Adam grew in his faith, he continued to be a witness to the other inmates. By his fourth year in prison he was leading the Bible study group and teaching other inmates to read. He also began to work with the prison Chaplain and Pastor Mark, and when she could be there, Nicole.

Nicole was always busy. It seemed as if she could handle anything life threw at her. She kept up her work on the anti-violence campaign and even wrangled permission from the prison superintendent to allow Adam to make his own public service announcement about the effects of domestic violence. Adam came across as compassionate and sincere. He spoke openly of what he had done and how much he regretted it. He talked about giving his life to Jesus. It was a powerful and simple message.

Meanwhile, Nicole finished her certification for Physical Therapy. She planned to open another gym. And of course, she was busy with four children, plus the fur babies, both dogs and horses.

She had a few models approach her asking her to manage their careers. Soon she opened a small modeling agency. Since she coached her models on professionalism along with modeling techniques, her models were well-liked and known in the industry for being extremely skilled.

Life was going well.

One day she was lying by the pool when a phone call came.

"Nicole, this is Superintendent Thompkins from the prison. I wanted to inform you that Adam Hannan was attacked in the yard. He needs surgery right away or he will not be expected to survive. Even with the surgery it will be touch and go. The problem is he refuses to go into surgery until he sees you. Please come as soon as you can."

"Troy," she called out, running upstairs to grab a dress, "Adam has been attacked, he might die and he's asking to see me. Will you drive me there?"

"Of course." He called Julia, who had stayed on with David and Emily.

Julia quickly came over to babysit the two youngest children. They packed the twins, who were now five years old, into their car seats, and started out. Along the way, Nicole pulled on the dress over her bathing suit, and then called Pastor Mark. He said he would leave right away and meet them there.

Upon arriving at the prison they were escorted inside without having to pass through all the security measures they usually had to go through. This bypassing of established protocol alone heightened Nicole's sense of urgency. When she got to the infirmary, all she could do was take Adam's hand and pray with him. He was very weak. He knew he should go into surgery but he wanted to see Nicole first. By the time Nicole and Troy arrived, the surgeon just shook his head.

"Too late," he said quietly.

Nicole was badly shaken. For a moment she could not find

the right words to speak.

Finally she managed to say, "You'll be with Jesus soon. It will be all right." Surprising even herself, there were tears on her cheeks. She held his hand and said the Lord's Prayer.

"I'm sorry," he managed to whisper, "for everything."

"What you did took a lot from me, but I forgave you long ago. Now I think of you as a good friend and a true Christian." She paused, thinking. "You took many things from me but you gave me a great gift, too. I have some new pictures to show you."

She pulled a picture from her purse. "Here are the beautiful son and daughter you gave me."

Adam was overcome at the pictures, they were getting so big! While he was staring at the images, she spoke to the prison superintendent.

"They are in the waiting room with my husband, would it be all right for him to bring them in?" she asked quietly.

"I'll send for them." He turned to a phone on the wall.

"Nicole," Adam managed, "are my children happy? Well loved?"

"Yes, Adam, they are happy and will be raised in love," she said softly. "I love them and so does Troy. He couldn't love them more if he was their real father. They are both bright and happy, and they will be raised to love Jesus."

Troy came in with the twins holding his hands. They had been playing outside when the call came in, so they were covered with dirt. They looked at Adam with some suspicion but they were confident children and walked right over to him when Nicole reached out a shaking and trembling hand to them. Upon their approaching the father they never had an opportunity to know, he gently stroked their hair.

"It's good." These were the last words he said while on this earth.

Troy took the children back out.

Pastor Mark and Rachel rushed in. They sat with Nicole and

prayed as Adam's breathing got rougher and slower. Rachel softly sang the old hymn, "How Great Thou Art." Adam gave a few more rasping breaths, then his breathing ceased.

Pastor Mark prayed, "Lord, please take this man who was first a prisoner to his false religion which had taught him to hate, and then a prisoner in this earthly prison that was the culmination of that hate. He is finally free of this earthly soil. Let him stand before our beloved Savior he has come to know and serve, even here in prison. He has repented of that horrific day where he took the life of Nicole's friends. This man is a trophy of grace. Take him home to meet his victims from that fateful day and share in the joys of heaven with them as they all walk arm in arm in praise to the King of kings."

Adam found himself being welcomed into heaven by Hans, Ivan and Lacey.

Two months later, Nicole went back to the prison to witness to the man who had killed Adam.

"Jesus said unto him, I am the way, the truth, and the life: no man comes to the Father, but by me."
(John 14:6)

Other books by Susan Kohler

The Heart of The Beast
(historical romance novel)

Working Romance
(contemporary romance novel)

Who's Taming Who?
(contemporary romance novel)

Dreaming of Tomorrow
(contemporary romance novel)

www.ingramcontent.com/pod-product-compliance
Lightning Source LLC
Chambersburg PA
CBHW020333260626
47156CB00004B/1501

Note to Readers

Please visit my website at:

http://sueotk2001.tripod.com/connectionpointewritings

I have excerpts and information on my novels.

Sue